bittersweet

D1280689

bittersweet
confessions of a twice-married man

PHILIP LEE

GOOSE LANE

Copyright © 2008 by Philip Lee.

All rights reserved. No part of this work may be reproduced or used in any form or by any means, electronic or mechanical, including photocopying, recording, or any retrieval system, without the prior written permission of the publisher or a licence from the Canadian Copyright Licensing Agency (Access Copyright). To contact Access Copyright, visit www.accesscopyright.ca or call 1-800-893-5777.

Edited by Bethany Gibson.
Cover photograph © Image Source/Corbis.
Cover and book design by Julie Scriver.
Printed in Canada on 100% PCW paper.
10 9 8 7 6 5 4 3 2 1

Library and Archives Canada Cataloguing in Publication

Lee, Philip J., 1963-
  Bittersweet: confessions of a twice-married man / Philip Lee.

Includes bibliographical references.
ISBN 978-0-86492-463-6

  1. Lee, Philip J., 1963- . 2. Divorced men — Canada — Biography.
I. Title.

PS8623.E4434B48 2008   C818'.603   C2008-903814-2

Goose Lane Editions acknowledges the financial support of the Canada Council for the Arts, the Government of Canada through the Book Publishing Industry Development Program (BPIDP), and the New Brunswick Department of Wellness, Culture, and Sport for its publishing activities.

Goose Lane Editions
Suite 330, 500 Beaverbrook Court
Fredericton, New Brunswick
CANADA E3B 5X4
www.gooselane.com

This is a work of non-fiction. All characters, places, and events are real. Wherever possible I have relied on interviews, references to journal entries, and other documents to recall events as accurately as possible. I am responsible for all mistakes of failing memory.

For Lucy

Eros the melter of limbs (now again) stirs me —
sweetbitter unmanageable creature who steals in

— Sappho

It was Sappho who first called eros "bittersweet."
No one who has been in love disputes her.

— Anne Carson

The Dark Year

1

On the summer afternoon I returned to the old house by the sea, I parked my car in the weeds by the back door and walked through a field of tall grasses and wildflowers to watch the incoming tide. I climbed down over the bank to the beach, where the waves splashed and rolled across polished stones and seaweed beds, where the air smelled of salt, sun, and the shore.

Here in the bay that Portuguese sailors named Rio Fundo, the "deep river," water washes in from the Gulf of Maine and crashes against the continental shelf, creating a special soup of gravity, depth, distance, and waves that produces the highest tides in the world. The Bay of Fundy shore is a place of constant motion. The tides are forever coming and going, forever rearranging the stones and gravel on the beach. When storm waters rise and the highest tides surge on the full moon, waves pound the cliffs. Whole pieces of the shore crumble and fall; and these rocks are broken again and scattered across the beach.

The tides here are a mighty force, but up close, in slow time, their movement is so unhurried that I sometimes forget the water is rising until another crevice is filled and another rock disappears, until the seaweed beds are floating and the waves are swirling at my feet. In this way, change washed into my life.

I stood at the edge of the water, watching the rising tide, then wandered down the beach, around the rocky point, and across the next beach until I turned and retraced my steps to the old house. I sat on the front porch and had a good long cry. All this crying was a new thing for me. As a young man, I had a stiff upper lip that I figure was passed down from my ancestors, the indefatigable Confederate fighters from the southern United States. Whenever I cried as a boy, my father used to tell me, "Son, get hold of yourself." Years later, he told me he regretted speaking those words, but he was repeating what his father had told him, and that we all, in ways great and small, bear the sins of our fathers. I took my father's words to heart and, as a young man, learned to get hold of myself. But when my marriage fell apart, I started crying.

In the weeks before I left the farm where I had been living with my wife and our three children, I would see the kids off to school in the mornings and then moments later, collapse sobbing, asking myself over and over, What have I done? What have I done? I would force myself to move, one foot in front of the other, until I had momentum, and I would hurry about the farm, feeding and watering our two horses and putting them out to pasture, running the two dogs, and shooing the cats out the back door and filling their bowls with food and water. I would wash my face and hands, put on my suit, knot my tie, and drive to work, listening to the morning news on the radio while I ran an electric razor over my chin and tried to turn my mind toward the tasks of the day — tasks that absorbed me and offered a measure of relief.

That summer afternoon when I arrived at the old house was the day I left the farm for good. I was thirty-five years old, and while I may not yet have reached mid-life, I was fully in crisis. I sat on the porch for a long time before I felt able to walk to the car, open the trunk, and carry my bags inside.

After the sun set behind the spruce trees on the point, I went upstairs and tried to sleep in the bedroom with the window that looks out to the sea, in the bed where my parents slept during the endless summers of my youth. I spent half the night lying awake in my parents' bed and half the night wandering through the house, smoking cigarettes and reading old paperback mystery novels.

When I came downstairs in the morning, dizzy from lack of sleep, I found three squirrels in the kitchen, one sitting on the table and two on the floor, regarding me with surprise, as if I were invading their space. I chased them out the back door, slammed it shut, and reminded myself that the old house needed a spring cleaning. Then I walked out the front door and stood on the wet grass in my bare feet and watched the ducks swim and dive in the cove. The sea was calm, the tide was rising again, and the waves were breaking softly on the beach. I dried my feet on the porch boards and climbed the stairs to dress for work.

2

I became a husband and a father in my early twenties and entered the period of life that American songwriter Greg Brown describes in his song "Worrisome Years." My wife and I were starting careers, living in apartments and rented homes, moving at least once a year, raising children and being broke, and wondering too often, "When does the good part start?"

I was a father of two little girls by the time I graduated from Dalhousie University in Halifax, Nova Scotia, with a master's degree in the classics. I could read ancient Greek, I had spent years exploring the pages of Homer's poetry and Plato's dialogues, but I had few skills that would help to support a family that to this point had been kept afloat by my wife's nursing job and my university scholarships. One day out of desperation, I took an aptitude test with an employment counsellor in downtown Halifax. He concluded that the only thing I could do well was write, and there wasn't much demand for writers. However, he did have an advertisement for a reporter's job at a small newspaper in a paper-mill town in central Newfoundland.

So I flew into Gander and drove an hour inland to the town of Grand Falls for a job interview at a biweekly newspaper called the *Advertiser*. I checked into the only hotel in town, ate my first meal of cod tongues at the hotel restaurant with the newspaper's overworked managing editor, who by the time we ordered coffee, offered me a job. I negotiated a salary of three hundred and fifty dollars a week, which was fifty dollars more than the newspaper paid most cub reporters, and then told him I needed to go home and talk it over with my wife. I returned to Halifax, and we decided to go Newfoundland. Perhaps there I would find the beginnings of a career and she would find work at the local hospital. We packed our family into our car, boarded the ferry in North Sydney, Nova Scotia, landed at Port aux Basques, and drove across the island through a blinding early fall snowstorm into a new life.

When I reported for work at the *Advertiser*, I discovered that I had a lot to learn about the newspaper business. And with an editorial staff of just three, including me, I had to learn in a hurry. At a small-town newspaper, taking photographs of the mayor at ribbon cuttings, the guest speaker at the Chamber of Commerce luncheon, and the winners of the high school science fair contest was half the job, and when I arrived, I didn't know how to load film into a 35-mm camera. My training session, which lasted all of half an hour, included a crash course in news writing and film loading.

We worked in a small cluster of offices built into the front of an industrial printing plant. On publication day, I would turn off my computer, walk out into the plant, pick up the printouts of the columns I had written, feed them through a waxing machine, and paste them onto pages. I proofread the pages, then sent them to be photographed, plated, and hung on the press. When the press rolled, the whole building shook, and I was back in my office planning the next edition.

Most days, I was too busy to stop and think about what I had got myself into, but I remember the day I realized I had stumbled by chance into the kind of work I really wanted to do. I had been assigned to cover the report of an inquiry into a forest fire ignited by sparks from a passing train — an event of great interest in a town whose economic survival depended on the local supply of timber that fed the mill. The report was all routine technical testimony, until I came upon a story told by the foreman of a logging crew. He and his men had been clearing a fire line near a logging camp when he realized the fire was racing toward them and they wouldn't be able to stop it or get out of its way. In moments he gathered the men in a clearing beside the camp and told them to hose down everything, including themselves. Then he instructed them to lie down on the wet ground. The fire passed over them. All survived.

In this man's account of leadership and courage, I found what I wanted to do with my life. When I wrote this kind of story for the newspaper, I was writing about the subjects that had interested me when I was reading Homer and Sophocles and Plato and contemplating what it means to live a life of virtue. Journalism, like poetry and philosophy, is an art that moves readers from particular images to universal ideas. Years later, one of my editors told me that the stories we were writing were like parables, little pictures, each in some way exploring the moral questions of our time.

I moved from the mill-town newspaper in central Newfoundland to a city newspaper in St. John's and learned the business of journalism from the inside out. Our son was born in the city, so then we were five. We bought our first home in a fishing village called Flatrock, on the outskirts of St. John's, and settled there on a wind-battered hill where we watched the waves of the North Atlantic explode against the rocks in the harbour below.

During the worrisome years, I considered myself an apprentice in a business where my value would always be judged by the last story I wrote. I set no boundaries for my work. I would spend long days at the office or on the road reporting, rush home to put dinner on the table because my wife was often working nights at the hospital, and then once the children were asleep and I had finished the household chores, I would turn on my computer and work into the late evening. I allowed my work to consume me. I never found a more balanced way of working as a journalist, although I knew my family wished I would learn to set limits. I was spending more time tending to the needs of my job than to the needs of my family. It would be many years before I learned to correct this imbalance.

I continued to work for newspapers and magazines, changing jobs for new opportunities, one of which took us back to the mainland. There, we hoped we might find the family home we had been searching for. That search, apart from my excessive work habits, had defined our lives during the worrisome years.

The search began during my final year of university, when our eldest daughter was a toddler, and we used to drive about the Nova Scotia countryside on weekends, visiting farms that were for sale. We inspected farmhouses, explored musty barns, waded through tall pasture grasses, and traversed old apple orchards, lugging our little girl in our arms or on my shoulders, imagining how we might make a home in these places. We never found a farm that had everything we wanted. We would inspect a property and on the drive home, conclude that the land wasn't flat enough, or the barns were beyond repair, or the house didn't have a large enough kitchen. Perhaps the deficiencies we found in these properties were just an excuse we gave ourselves to keep looking.

Some evenings, when we arrived home after dark to the cottage we were renting on the shore of St. Margarets Bay, tired and hungry with a sleeping child in the back seat, I would scold myself for wasting a precious summer day on a search I knew was pointless at this stage in our lives when instead I should have been out looking for a job. Then the next weekend we would be back at it again, real estate listings and maps spread out on the dashboard as we drove down lonely country roads, longing for something we didn't have, unable even to articulate what it was we were hoping to find.

The search carried me a long way, from the meadows of Nova Scotia's southern shore to the rocky coastline of Newfoundland to the valley of the St. John River in New Brunswick. I thought that finding the right place to live was the key to constructing a happy life, that when we arrived at our family home, wherever that might be, we would open the door and find ourselves standing there — happy.

We believed that our farm in the St. John River valley was the place we had been searching for, and we had admired it from a distance long before we liquidated everything we had to secure it. At the time, we were living a short walk down the road in an old storey-and-a-half house on a fifty-acre hillside lot, but we saw a better life on this old farm set back from the main road, with sweeping meadows and acres of mature forest. During our walks on a logging road that bordered the property, we got to know the owners of the farm, and when they decided to sell, we were able to buy it before it went on the market.

I am now convinced that when Leo Tolstoy wrote that every happy family is alike and every unhappy family is unhappy in its own way, he had it only half right. Every happy family is also happy in its own way. I think Tolstoy understood this as well, because in his great novel of the family, he is most fascinated by the exquisite character of Anna Karenina and her pursuit of love and happiness after she leaves her husband, Levin. Despite the tragic nature of Anna's pursuit and the redemption of Levin late in the novel, we are left without a satisfactory resolution to the juxtaposition of what Tolstoy regards as the objective good of marriage and family and the subjective wonders of love. For many of us, the question of how we find happiness in this life turns on the possibility that at some point we will form a union with another person, and perhaps create a family, and find love all in the same place.

We moved into the farm with high hopes. We renovated the house and barns, fenced in pastures, always making plans and looking ahead. Our children played in the fields and forests and made a playhouse in an old cottage on the property. My wife brought in horses and I planted gardens and cut firewood. In the winter, we skied across the meadows and up and down the trails through the woods.

For the first time in my life, I was finding some balance between my life at work and my life at home. I had left the newspaper business and was editor of a monthly fishing and river conservation magazine, a job that allowed me to work in my home office about half the time and to go fly fishing in spring, summer, and fall, and call it research.

I didn't pause often for self reflection in those days, but at some point, I realized that no matter how close we came to creating the family home we had imagined as newlyweds, nothing about ourselves had changed. There was nowhere else to look, no more maps or real estate listings. It wasn't easy to admit this to myself, but there it was: the search had run its course.

One day, I took a phone call from the manager of a local newspaper. We had a meeting, and I left the fishing magazine and returned to the daily grind. I put away my fly rod and began working longer hours than I ever had, stepping right back into the patterns I had developed in the early years of our marriage. As a result, my wife and children were unhappy with me, and I had no one to blame but myself. I was responsible for my work habits, my state of mind — and for not articulating my unhappiness to either my wife or myself.

3

I was running so fast and so blind that the feelings caught me by surprise. I realized I was in trouble one day when I was thinking about her as I walked alone on the back forty of the farm. It was then that I called my younger sister, Susan, at her home in Ottawa and told her I was falling for another woman.

Susan is a listener, the sibling who binds my brother and sisters together, the sister who invariably shows up at our doors, suitcase in hand, when one of us is experiencing some kind of crisis. Susan listened to me talk, recognized that I had entered dangerous territory, and promised to call me every day. She told me to try not to fear what was happening, that sometimes the life we have constructed needs to fall apart before we are able to begin the process of making something better. She added this caveat: if you need to change your life, try to understand why. The understanding was a long time coming.

Essayist and magazine editor Lewis Lapham maintains that the task of a storyteller is to draw the wilderness of our experience within the fence posts of a beginning, middle, and end. He writes that the truth of a story and the voice of the author emerge from "the struggle to get at the truth of what he or she thinks, has seen, remembers, can find language to express." Almost a decade after that summer afternoon when I returned to the old house by the sea, I began to write the story of what had happened to me after my marriage ended. In the struggle to find the language to express it, I began to understand what had happened during the years I reconstructed my life.

From the outset, I set a condition for myself: I would not tell the story of my first marriage or the story of our divorce. That story was not mine alone to tell, unless I were to tell only one side of it; and I learned long ago in my little newspaper office in Newfoundland that there is never only one side to a story. By necessity my version would be incomplete. I didn't want to present a distorted picture of the life we lived, which the divorce wars so often do. I didn't want to lose sight of the simple truth that we had many successes in this marriage that is now, in the language of divorce, called a failure, the greatest of which was becoming the parents of three beautiful and wise children.

When we started out, we were so young, compatible in some areas of our lives and incompatible in others. She was my heroic partner in all the ways, large and small, in which parents strive to make a home for their children and keep them safe and happy. To assign a value to this kind of history, to point to this or that as good or bad or right or wrong, is to try to pass judgment on that which can't be judged.

My experience is that of a particular man in a singular place and time, and I can't offer universal answers to questions about love and marriage. What I can offer is my little picture, my report back from the road of second chances.

As I wrote this story, I repeatedly found myself demanding another level of honesty, and from time to time, I would check to see whether my words passed the sister test. When I thought I had found an honest narrative line, I would run it past Susan, and more often than not, she would tell me that I needed to go back and "unpack that a little more."

One weekend when I was wrestling with these matters, I went camping with Susan and her partner, Michel Thériault, who is a singer and songwriter from Acadian New Brunswick. The first night when we were drinking beer, feeding sticks into the fire, and trading songs on our guitars, Michel started playing a medley of what he called his "bad songs." One of these, which was written not to be recorded but as a bar song to be played at the end of the night, begins:

I'm just a regular asshole
I'm just a fuckin' jerk
I'm just a coward and a pig
I'm just un bon à rien

By the time he finished the first verse, we were all falling off our folding chairs in laughter. The next morning, I was humming the "regular asshole" song and thinking about the story of my life after I returned to the old house by the sea. We laughed at Michel's song because, of course, it's true. I'm just a regular asshole and "un bon à rien," a good for nothing, not all the time but some of the time to be sure. We're all just regular assholes at various times in our lives, some of us more than others. But we are offered an opportunity in this life to lift ourselves up — and be lifted up — when we participate in what poet Elizabeth Barrett Browning called "the great work of love."

4

My grandfather, my father's father and my namesake, is the one who discovered the old house. He was a railroad man from the southern United States, a self-made success who as a fourteen-year-old boy began his working life sweeping the train station in Elba, Alabama. When he was sixteen, he landed a job as a travelling freight agent for Atlantic Coastline Railroad and moved to Savannah, Georgia, where he found a room in the big city and ate bananas and crackers and drank water until he received his first pay. Years later, as a railroad vice-president, he travelled up and down the eastern seaboard in a private car staffed with a cook and a porter. Pa never forgot his humble beginnings in the working world, and would always tell his children and grandchildren about the nutritional and economical advantages of bananas and crackers when times get tough.

He was a tall, thin man who wore fine hats to cover his bald head and conducted his affairs with the mannerisms of a southern gentleman. Pa chose his words carefully and was unfailingly polite, even if he disagreed with every word someone said, which he often did. In the business world, he was innovative and tough. He drove his cars too fast and suffered from debilitating migraines that we attributed to stress. He adored his grandchildren, and when I was in the room, he was always gentle — both in speech and touch. He called me "son" and pulled me onto his lap and held me close so he could speak to me in a soft voice.

Soon after my parents — both natives of the southern United States — settled with their four children in the port city of Saint John, New Brunswick, my grandfather began searching for coastal real estate, a place on the shore where he could stay with his son and daughter-in-law and his grandchildren during his summer visits to Eastern Canada. Pa had seen many miles of coastal land and knew a place of beauty when he saw one. I was a six-year-old boy tagging along with his grandfather the day Pa discovered the old house in a fishing and clam digging community south of Saint John.

We had spent the morning driving along the shore looking at available waterfront properties, and the old house was our last stop. We parked by the beach and started walking together up the lane to the house. Pa was holding my hand when we encountered a large growling and barking black dog that appeared to be guarding the house. Pa stopped in his tracks, sized up the dog, and without a word, retreated to the beach where he picked up a stick of driftwood and gave it a few test swings. With the stick in his right hand and my hand in his left, he kept the dog at bay as we walked up the lane to the house. There, we discovered that the dog was protecting a cat and its litter of new kittens in a back shed, and that if we kept our distance from the dog's adopted family we were free to roam around the house. As we walked back to the car, Pa told me, "Son, a man never has to fear a dog so long as the man is carrying a big stick."

I thought about my Pa during the first days after my return to the old house. I remembered the barking dog and the big stick and knew that at some point I had to start facing my fears, of which I had many. I was afraid that a divorce would permanently damage my relationship with my children, that I would no longer be able to be the kind of father I wanted them to have in their lives. I was afraid of causing them more pain, because I knew they were already suffering enormous sadness because of the division of the family. I was also consumed by guilt, the first cousin of fear, because I had caused our marriage to end and I had hurt my wife in the process.

I remembered how Pa believed in facing our fears head on, and I decided that the old house was as good a place as any to do that. This was the place where, as a boy, I had learned to rely on myself during the summers when our family moved here from the city. It was here that I was free to explore the shore and the limits of my imagination. It was here I learned to row a boat and catch, clean, and cook fish, to climb cliffs and swim in cold water, to read the kinds of books I wanted to read, to play guitar and sing. Perhaps here, as a man, I could learn how to rebuild my life.

However, facing my fears when I returned to the old house that summer wasn't as easy as finding a big stick and marching forward past a barking dog, for the fear and guilt had settled firmly inside me. They rolled around in my mind during the day, formed a permanent knot in my gut, and kept me from sleeping at night. Guilt and fear can stop a man in his tracks. I couldn't see a way past them.

5

She worked with me at the newspaper I edited, and it was there that we became friends. I appreciated her writing and her work as a reporter and editor, and depended on her in the newsroom. Deb Nobes is a confident woman who believes in herself and trusts her judgment; she didn't hesitate to correct me when she thought I was making mistakes or to encourage me when she thought I was making good decisions. She had no hidden agenda, just a true and sincere focus on the task at hand, which is all a person can ask of another in the tense and deadline-driven news business. Surely E.B. White, who fell in love with Katherine Sergeant Angell, the literary editor at the *New Yorker*, where he worked, had this kind of friendship in mind when he composed the penultimate line in his famous children's book *Charlotte's Web*: "It is not often that someone comes along who is a true friend and a good writer." Deb was both.

I began to let my guard down when we were together, and in the moments when we found ourselves away from deadlines, our conversations drifted into areas other than work. She had studied journalism at the University of King's College, across from the Dalhousie University campus where I had studied classics. She had arrived in Newfoundland shortly after I left and had lived on the same piece of coastline where we had lived on the outskirts of St. John's. She had worked in the same newspaper office where I had spent long hours as a young reporter. In the beginning, I allowed myself to acknowledge that she was a good friend and that I felt better when she was around. Then I started to feel dizzy and disoriented when she walked into the room.

I was finding her beautiful in every respect. She is tall and slender, with straight, thick, dark hair and startlingly bright blue eyes that remind me of the shifting translucent blues in the sun-drenched Mediterranean Sea. I found myself admiring her eyes and her long fingers, the way her clothes hung on her shoulders, the way her feet fit in her shoes, the sound of her voice when she read me passages from the morning newspaper.

One Saturday afternoon in the spring, a couple of months before I returned to the old house, we both ended up at the newspaper office dressed in our jeans and sneakers to catch up on some work on the one down day of the news cycle. We sat on opposite sides of my desk (piled high with old newspapers and printouts of the previous night's work on the weekend edition), looked at each other for a long moment, and mumbled something like, "Well, what the hell are we going to do about this?" She had been thinking about me too and was facing complications of her own, notably a common-law relationship of six years with another reporter at the newspaper.

One morning a few weeks later, without even knowing for sure I was going to do it until the words spilled out of my mouth, I told my wife I was having feelings for another woman. At the time, and for a long time afterwards, I told myself this was the honourable thing to do. I needed to level with my wife because this had happened to me, the feelings were real, right there in front of me every day, and we had to face them. There is truth in that. However, in hindsight, my decision to spill without thinking through the consequences, without a plan for what would happen after I spoke the words, was terribly naive and reckless. None of my rationalizations after the fact could dull the excruciating pain and hurt and betrayal I delivered to my wife that morning. I invited chaos and turmoil into our household, not anticipating how profoundly the lives of my children would change and how deeply the people I loved most would suffer.

To make matters worse, our story soon entered the public domain, and because Deb and I worked together, the story became exaggerated and was discussed and embellished by gossips around water coolers in the office and at lunch counters downtown. When Deb and her partner separated and divided their possessions, our story even warranted a paragraph in the newsroom gossip section of a national muckraking magazine. In the end, it wasn't much of a scandal because I had spilled before we had a chance to do anything beyond admit we had feelings for each other. However, this mess of a beginning was hardly a fairy-tale romance. There were many days when Deb thought she might walk away, make a new start somewhere else, and leave me behind. I wouldn't have blamed her if she had. Less than a month later, I had moved into the house on the Bay of Fundy shore.

6

The old house makes a grand statement, facing the sea with its plumb and solid bones and green-hipped roof. It sits on the rocky high ground between a salt marsh and the clam flats, at the head of a point of land that juts out into the bay, where it can be seen from many vantage points along the coast. Captains of scallop draggers use the old house as a reference point when they are marking their trawls miles out at sea.

Inside, not much had changed since my grandfather closed the deal. Most of the furniture came with the house. There were whitewashed cupboards in the kitchen and an embroidered settee and chair in the front parlour, a big oval table in the dining room, and hand-carved hardwood beds and dressers in the bedrooms. Most of the floors were covered with faded linoleum. My parents had refinished the wooden floor in the living room, done some painting, and hung new wallpaper in the kitchen, which had become as faded and tattered as the wallpaper in the rest of the house. There was a hand pump in the kitchen and an outhouse connected to the shed in the backyard. It was a two-seater, with a smaller seat and step for children that my parents built when we were young. At the back of the house, there was a system for collecting rain off the roof in barrels that was piped into the backroom and connected to a sink and shower stall. There was a wood cookstove in the kitchen and an antique two-burner electric camp stove in the backroom. It had two settings: red hot high and off. Collections of green, blue, and white sea glass were piled on the windowsills in every room.

Walter and Augusta McPherson built the house in the early

1900s, ferrying building materials by boat before a road had been cut from the village to the point. The majority of the houses in the village were raised around the sheltered clam flats in the basin, but the McPhersons were fishermen, not diggers, and they imagined a homestead closer to the open sea, even if it was more isolated and exposed to the wind and waves. Walter and Augusta raised six children in the house on the point and lived there until they were in their nineties, when they died within months of each other.

I remember standing in the kitchen when Allan McPherson, who had been born in one of the upstairs bedrooms, stomped in through the back door, his big wading boots folded down at the knee, and spilled a bucket of live lobsters on the kitchen table as a housewarming gift. Until he fell ill in the final years of his life, Allan drove almost every day to the point — McPherson's Point, as it will always be called — and stood on the beach to watch the tide wash upon the shore of his youth.

In the evenings after I returned to the old house, I would stand for a moment in the place where Allan McPherson had stood, to re-establish my equilibrium in the presence of the predictable motions of the tides, in the presence of something constant. This was unending motion to be sure, but as Greek philosopher Heraclitus argued, motion and change have an underlying universal order, or *logos*. The ancient Greeks understood that most of us are walking around blind through the confusion of apparently random events in our daily lives, simply because that is the human condition. However, they believed that events are not random but connected to an unchanging divine order. For Homer, the *logos* was the order of Zeus. For Plato, the *logos* was what he called "The Good." That's why the Greeks looked for the presence of gods all around them, in the waves, in the clouds and the thunder, in an eagle riding the winds, circling in the sky. The Greeks, unlike so many of us who wander in the wilderness of the modern world, never felt completely isolated from a divine order.

If Odysseus, the hero of one of literature's great love stories, were walking in my shoes, he would have believed that some god had led him back to the old house, and he would have stood by the shore where Allan McPherson watched the tides and searched for a sign. He would have fallen to his knees and asked if he was on a course sanctioned by the gods. The gods showed me no signs, at least none that I could discern, but I kept looking, and watching the tides, and searching, for what I didn't know, but it was all I could figure to do.

7

Two uninhabited islands called The Brothers lie about a mile offshore from the old house. Their cliffs and rocky beaches have been shaped and smoothed by the tides and currents in the bay. On the clearest blue days, we can see the islands of Grand Manan, Campobello, and the Wolves as dark strips and hills that float and shimmer on the distant horizon. The Brothers, however, are our islands, and they never disappear from our view except on days when the thickest fog settles over the point. We do know that many years ago, long before anyone can remember, the two islands were one, until the waves washed over a narrow isthmus and cracked the rocks and pushed the debris into the sea to make them two. We know this because ever since we have been watching The Brothers they have been connected by a long sandbar that emerges at low tide — allowing us to imagine what was — before the bar slips below the surface when the waters rise.

When we were children, we named the islands Walter and Philip, the larger island on the right named for me, and the smaller island on the left for my brother, who is five years younger and in those days was smaller in stature. Some years after we personalized The Brothers, our family took a trip on a fishing boat out beyond the islands and discovered that the Walter island is in fact larger than the Philip island, the long backside of the Walter island being hidden from our usual view. We learned how fallible our senses are, how little we know about the world around us, even about perceptions that we believed were correct and unassailable.

During my first weeks at the old house, everything about my future was uncertain, except that I wouldn't be living there alone, because Walter had come to the house a few weeks before I had. His marriage was also ending. He had been living in a farmhouse about a half an hour away, and his wife was in the process of packing up and moving to Ontario. He was travelling in Vietnam and Japan on a student-recruiting mission for the University of New Brunswick, a contract he had recently landed, and before boarding his plane, he had dropped off some of his belongings. Just inside the front door, I found his piles of cardboard boxes and duffel bags. Some of the contents had been unpacked and stacked on the floor.

Walter and I were roommates as children and became best friends as men. Siblings don't always become friends, and I consider his friendship one of the joys of my life. During my worrisome years, before Walter was married, he would show up at our place from time to time with a case of beer and we would stay up all night talking. I would encourage him to continue the conversation long after he wanted to sleep because I was hungry for the contact with an adult outside my little family enclosure. Once, I flew from St. John's to spend the weekend in Halifax, where Walter was then living, and after I finished my business in the city, he and I stayed up for thirty-six hours straight, got drunk, and then sobered up and continued our conversation until I had to leave for the airport.

Like our father, Walter is a small man who stands five feet, eight inches tall. Although he is about an inch shorter than I am, he is stockier and much stronger. He has blond hair and blue eyes and I have darker hair and my mother's brown eyes. When he was a younger man, Walter lived fast and hard, drank too much, and fought outside bars. Eventually, he recognized that he was caught in a life-and-death struggle with himself, so he stopped getting drunk and seeking out fights and began searching for a better way to live.

He graduated from university with a degree in English literature and then travelled the country working as a labourer, including a stint on a salmon farm on the east coast. Walter is an expansive thinker, and as his mind was occupied with the broad movements of history, the details of the job site would sometimes slip past him. One day at the end of his shift, he motored into shore from the cages and tied the fibreglass dingy to his truck so he could pull it up the beach to store it above the head of tide. Sometime during the short drive up the beach, his mind turned to more important matters and he kept driving, waving and smiling at people along the side of the road, until he realized that they were pointing and laughing, and he looked in his rear-view mirror to find the dingy still at the end of its rope, bouncing along the pavement. He pulled over and dragged the boat up over the tailgate of his truck, returned to the beach to deposit it in its berth, and drove home laughing at himself, as he would later during the telling of the story.

Before he left for Asia, Walter and his wife met for coffee and wrote out a separation agreement on a slip of paper. For most of their short marriage they had been either travelling the world or homesteading, two ways of living that will either bind a couple together or drive them apart. They took their shiny new marriage right out of the showroom and drove it around the world at top speed, not allowing for a breaking-in period. Some marriages can survive that kind of treatment; others will seize up. When Walter and his wife finally tried to settle in one place, they couldn't get the marriage working right again. So they met for coffee and went their separate ways.

It was a clean break, except that Walter had to kill the chickens. Neither he nor his wife knew anything about farming, but they had decided that a simplified life would be an honest and responsible way for them to live, so they moved into an old homestead at the end of a long country road. The house, which was in ruins, belonged to a friend of Walter's. They planned to restore the house and reclaim the fields and gardens, which were wild and overgrown. All the while they would learn to grow food, to maintain a household without running water or appliances, and to build and use a composting toilet. It was an ambitious plan, and they achieved many things before the enterprise was abandoned, including the renovation of the downstairs of the house, the construction of the toilet, the planting of a garden, and the purchase of chickens so they could eat fresh eggs. When the marriage broke down, the homesteading enterprise dissolved, and they both decided to leave the farmhouse, which remained vacant for a long time afterwards.

When Walter and his wife parted ways, the chickens were still foraging on the property, and it fell to my brother to deal with them. He went back to the farm, shot and buried the mean old rooster, captured the chickens, and brought them in his truck to the old house, where he wrung their necks, gutted, plucked, bagged, and froze them. Walter told me later as he described the bloody scene in the backyard of the old house: "I thought to myself, Well, here we are, here we are then. *That* was closure."

When Walter returned from Asia, I moved to the back bedroom where my older sister, Sadie, used to sleep. My brother had arrived first and therefore had first choice of bedrooms. He had chosen the front one. I moved without objection or discussion; as siblings, we had worked these kinds of rules out years ago. My new room had a single window that looked out over a tidal creek, salt marsh, and pond. I slept on a wooden bed that came with the house and now had a mattress and futon stacked on top of each other, the effect of which was to create a soft crater in the centre. There was an antique hardwood dresser in the corner with a mirror so stained I could no longer see my reflection in the glass.

I hung my three suits and a week's worth of dry cleaned shirts on a clothes rack that my father built when I was a boy. My father is a Presbyterian minister and a fine theologian, but one of the most unhandy men I have ever met. He never had the right tools or materials for the job at hand and only visited hardware stores and lumberyards as a last resort. If he was replacing deck boards on the front porch he would search the property for a board, perhaps one that had washed up on the beach that was a close fit, preferably one that didn't need to be cut, and then he would find his box of rusty bent nails and would straighten each one before pounding it in. This was the Protestant work ethic run amok, the belief that if we only applied ourselves, the bent nails and the imperfect board would do the job just fine. So the clothes rack was poorly designed, constructed with driftwood poles, and nailed together with some of his bent nails. It sagged and leaned in the corner and only stood straight if the clothes were balanced right in the centre.

34

Apart from being a poor handyman, my father is my role model in many other areas of life. He keeps a photograph of our ancestor Robert E. Lee, along with a framed letter written by the general, on the wall in his study, beside the photograph of another one of his heroes, Abraham Lincoln. The Lincoln photograph is important to my father, who was raised on white supremacy and Dixie patriotism but learned as a young man the difference between good and evil disguised as good. Before my parents left the United States and brought their family to Canada in early 1969, my father and mother became active in the civil rights movement, participating in marches for racial justice in the South. My father is a great admirer of Lincoln, in particular his theology, despite the fact that Lincoln never participated in organized religion. He particularly admires his second inaugural address, when Lincoln suggested that perhaps the institution of slavery and the Civil War were part of God's design for America. God first willed these sins upon the nation and then willed that they be removed. The war was the terrible price of redemption.

My father taught me that General Lee's genius was expressed in retreat. Lee led his army north into Pennsylvania, lost the battle at Gettysburg, then retreated south, punishing the pursuing Union army in a series of bloodbaths during the next two years. I would often think of Lee when I was trying to decide whether to stand and fight, which is usually my first instinct, or to retreat and regroup to fight another day. Years later, I recognized that my return to the old house was a strategic retreat, a place for regrouping until I was ready to begin a march forward again.

I don't know how to explain the coincidence that brought my brother and me back together at the family home created by our grandparents and parents. I know they never imagined their summer retreat would be occupied by two brothers working their way through broken marriages. We needed a roof over our heads, but more than that we needed each other. We grieved our losses and were both frightened by our uncertain futures. Years later, my brother and I would recall our time together at the old house, first with forced smiles, and eventually we would laugh until we were wiping away tears. But back then, we weren't laughing. We would come to call our time together at the old house "the dark year."

8

After I left the family farm, I spent as much time as possible with my children. My daughters, Danielle and Gabrielle, were fourteen and twelve, and my son, Aaron, was nine. When they visited the old house on weekends, the girls slept together in one of the upstairs bedrooms where they had stayed as young children. Aaron slept with me. They loved the house and the shore. They played house in a little cabin I had built as a boy in the woods, and we explored the beaches at low tide and went swimming in the icy waters of the bay. In the evenings, we rented movies from a nearby gas station, made popcorn, and retreated into the safety of familiar love.

Danielle has sunset-red hair and blue-sky eyes that she inherited from her distant Irish ancestors. She smiles and laughs easily, has a quick and brilliant mind, and is a voracious reader. She possesses a kind of rare intellect that allows her to understand science and math, read and interpret literature, write well, and create art. I once saw a boxing match between an American woman and an Irish woman as the under card to a title match I was watching with friends. The American fighter, stocky and fast, was winning from the opening bell, but her wiry Irish opponent fought back with grace and courage; she got up off the mat more than once to bloody the nose of the American and won her respect before losing on points. I remembered that match long after the title fight was forgotten, because that young Irish woman, with her red hair and freckles and indomitable spirit, reminded me of Danielle. During the dark year, Danielle refused to be defeated. She tried to bring order to the chaos of the old house, sweeping floors and rearranging the cluttered kitchen. Some evenings, she organized missions to get takeout pizza or fish and chips from local diners. As the oldest child, the leader, she was determined to guide her siblings through the difficult days.

Gabby, with deep, dark eyes and brown hair, looks nothing like her sister and carries within her a different kind of strength. She has a pure, immediate sense of empathy and compassion and at the same time is the most strong-willed person I have ever met. I have come to respect and admire this middle daughter's I-won't-back-down spirit that I've been contending with since before she was old enough to speak. That summer, Gabby led us on walks across the beaches at low tide. One of the challenges of taking walks with Gabby is that she refuses to retrace her steps. So morning walks would often last for hours as we picked our way along the shore, with Aaron riding on my back when he got tired. We would end up on some far-distant beach and climb up a bank onto the road to begin our long inland walk back to the house, all of us complaining about being tired, except Gabby, who was smugly satisfied that we were not walking over old ground. For Gabby, nothing ruins a good walk more than turning back.

Aaron in those days was my baby, soft and gentle, all blond hair and blue eyes, wanting to grow up and compete with his sisters but clinging to me at the same time. He wasn't talking about what had happened to the family but was watching his parents and sisters closely, keeping his fears hidden. He slept with me at night, he said, not because he was afraid but because he didn't like to sleep alone. I held his little body close to mine long after he had fallen asleep, and I lay awake worrying about how these children were really coping, how they might be damaged in the long term by what had happened to their family. More than anything I wanted to find a way to be a better father, and a better man.

9

After I moved into the old house, I began seeking spiritual guidance from a family friend, a Roman Catholic priest named Michael LeBlanc, who served in the west-side neighbourhood of Saint John where I grew up. He would drop by my parents' house, plunk himself down in a big armchair in the living room, accept my father's offer of a drink, and inspire hours of good conversation and laughter. When he moved to other parishes, he still visited and sometimes drove to the shore to spend time with us in the summer. I think our home allowed him to participate in the life of a family, with children running about and loud dinners and wide-ranging conversations that were missing in the quiet peace of the rectory. In return, he offered us his friendship.

Now it was my turn to drop in on him. I sat in a big armchair in Father Michael's living room in the rectory beside his new church in a Saint John suburb and told him how I had fallen for Deb, and that I had told my wife, and that my marriage had ended, and that I didn't know how to pick up the pieces of my family and begin to rebuild my life.

Father Michael said my mistake was not that I'd fallen in love. I shouldn't feel badly about that. I was open to love, which was a good thing. What was her name? He kept forgetting. Debbie? Well, she could be Debbie or Cheryl, her name didn't really matter, he said. The relevant fact was that I was open to these feelings. She filled a hole that needed to be filled. This love might last, or perhaps I would find someone else. If I had made any mistake, it had been telling my wife about my feelings before I knew what I was going to do. That was irresponsible. Why didn't I come to see him months ago?

I asked him why, with such strong role models as my parents, Walter and I were now living together in the old house. Father Michael shook his head sadly. My parents were terrible role models for me and my brothers and sisters when it came to marriage, he told me, precisely because they had found and nurtured a lifelong love.

My parents met in Boston, where my mother, who graduated from Yale University with a master's degree in English, was being interviewed for a job to teach high school English and my father was finishing his studies at Harvard Divinity School, after which he would be ordained as a Presbyterian minister. They fell in love and married a year later. My mother stopped teaching and became a homemaker when my father began his ministry in Florida and then a full-time mother when my older sister, Sadie, was born. From there they moved to North Carolina, then to Maryland, where I was born, along with my younger sister, Susan, and brother, Walter. When I was five years old, we moved to New Brunswick. My father's church in downtown Saint John was a gathering place for Scottish immigrants, who loved my father for his sharp intellect, compassion, and principled inner core. They stood beside him for more than two decades, a small, fierce army of highlanders and lowlanders who followed my father into his battles inside and outside the church. My mother was the church's social ambassador, fixer of hurt feelings, babysitter of difficult children, and general unpaid partner in the mission. She also acted as a sounding board for my father's sermons, and she edited my father's writing. She returned to teaching only after her four children had graduated from high school.

What was perhaps atypical of an arrangement that appeared on the surface to conform to the classic 1950s nuclear family was that my parents were equal partners and shared in all decisions about the household. My father respected my mother's views and insisted that their children show her the respect and consideration she deserved. The one sin in our household that always drew an immediate rebuke from my father was showing disrespect to our mother. My mother managed the household finances, and over the years, they renegotiated their roles in the household, with my father taking on more domestic duties, such as cooking and cleaning, especially after my mother returned to work.

Father Michael told me that my father and mother had found a way to grow together as partners in the marriage. They had survived the worrisome years, had at various points renegotiated the union, and came out the other side still holding on to each other. He said we, their children, would always struggle to find a partnership that would live up to what we believed was ordinary but was, in fact, extraordinary.

Father Michael didn't advise me about how to proceed, other than to tell me to make sure I continued to see my children and to remind them that I would be there for them always. He told me to embrace what was happening to me as an opportunity for spiritual growth, that I had a chance to become a better father and a man who would learn to truly experience love. Living and loving is all about spiritual growth, he said. There is nothing else.

My parents had found a lasting love in marriage, but there is nothing inherent in the institution of marriage that helps us find that kind of love. There has also been a revolution in the institution of marriage since my parents began their life together in the late 1950s. In her eye-opening book, *Marriage, a History: From Obedience to Intimacy, or How Love Conquered Marriage*, Stephanie Coontz argues that the economic, political, social, and legal changes in marriage and in gender roles that emerged in the 1960s and 1970s have forever transformed the institution of marriage, for better or for worse.

People's hope that in marriage they will find love and friendship, and live happily ever after, is not new. This is the narrative line of Greek epics and fairy tales and Jane Austen novels. It's what most interested Jane Austen in *Pride and Prejudice* and what she embodied in the marvellous character of Lizzy Bennet, who is unwilling to settle for marriage without a multilayered love. Philosopher Allan Bloom writes in his analysis of *Pride and Prejudice* that "Jane Austen presents a reasonable picture of what may be an unreasonable hope, that is, the harmonious union of sexual desire with love, marriage and friendship."

Regardless of whether we believe this is a reasonable or unreasonable hope, what has changed is that we have joined these all-encompassing expectations for marriage with the legal ability to cut our losses should marriage fail to meet them. In marriage, we expect to find love, a partner for life, happiness, perhaps children, and financial, sexual, and personal fulfillment. We want it all.

While conservative critics often bemoan the fact that the institution of marriage is no longer valued, those of us who grew up in the age of no-fault divorce hold marriage in the highest esteem. The essential instability of marriage has its origins in our expectations. Falling in love and getting married is easy; finding lifelong love and personal happiness and fulfillment on every level within a marriage is an entirely different matter.

The difficulty is that we are still getting married with assumptions and rituals that no longer apply in this unstable territory. Many of us still say the words "till death do us part," "for better or for worse," when, in fact, they no longer reflect the nature of the marriage contract. We're in it for the better but not necessarily for the worse. Divorce statistics are contentious, but it is fair to say that about half of all first marriages in the western world end in divorce, and the likelihood of divorce increases with a second marriage, and increases again with a third and fourth marriage. If the enterprise of finding lasting love and marriage were subject to performance evaluations, value-for-money audits, or annual reviews, we would have shut down this failing human project some years ago.

What other legal contract do we enter into that carries such high expectations, that has no guidelines or measures of success, that is by nature tenuous and unstable, and that can be broken by either party without grounds? Why is it that when this fragile contract fails, the consequences are so poorly defined that we are expected, more often than not, to hire lawyers to help us reach a fair settlement?

Why do so many of us take for granted that we have entered a lifelong contract? Why do we think the work of nurturing the relationship, of making the contract work, ends the moment we say "I do" — despite the fact that these words merely signal the first small step in a long-term project?

Moreover, my generation's ideas of what a loving and peaceful household should be are clouded and confused by the pervasive images of the 1950s nuclear family — the male breadwinner–female homemaker partnership of my youth — even though this kind of household organization has been widely rejected by women and men and, in fact, is unsustainable in the modern economy. Nonetheless, some women often feel guilty when they don't stay home with the kids and some men still tend to put their careers first, leaving household management and domestic chores to their wives, even though they claim to understand that marriage must be an equal partnership. I was guilty of making the assumption that my newspaper career came first, and for years, we packed the family caravan and followed the multitude of opportunities that I found in the world of journalism. My family adjusted their aspirations to fit with mine.

All of us, men and women, are just a little confused as we try to navigate what Coontz calls "the perfect storm" of legal reforms and changes in personal and social expectations that swept through the institution of marriage during the last three decades of the twentieth century. "Like it or not, today we are all pioneers, picking our way through uncharted and unstable territory," she writes. When pioneers become lost, they have no one to turn to but themselves to find their way home.

11

During the first weeks and months of the dark year, I wasn't going anywhere, but I was always on the move. I often got up early and drove to the farm to get the kids off to school, or I went there in the evenings to prepare meals and help with homework when their mom was at work. I saw my children almost every day, and if I had sometimes taken them for granted in the past, I promised myself that I would never take them for granted again. I tried to do what I could to help maintain the farm, washing dishes and mowing the grass when I was there. Every time I came or went, I would feel the loss and the disorientation of not really living anywhere.

I embraced this displacement because I was afraid of what the consequences of restarting my life might be. Some of the fear was related to practical concerns. Where would I live? What kind of parenting arrangement would I have with my former wife? Some of the fear was related to my guilt. How could I allow myself to seek happiness in my life when the members of my family were suffering because of my actions?

This approach to living, which is not really living at all, is what I brought to the old house. Meanwhile, Walter was settling in as well as a man who had never really settled anywhere could. He recognized that I was doing the bare minimum to subsist, sleeping in the old house, eating at bad restaurants, and showering at my parents' home in the city after work. My shirts and suits went to the dry cleaners, my dirty clothes to the laundromat drop-off service. I wasn't changing the sheets on my bed and hadn't done the spring cleaning or bothered to deal with the squirrels that still had the run of the house.

Walter's first innovation was coffee in the mornings. He wanted us to be able to sit down and share a morning coffee. He found a stovetop espresso maker in one of his duffel bags, and with a blow-torch that he had dug out of a pile of junk in the backroom, we boiled coffee one cup at a time. He bought cream and stocked the fridge and split wood to cook on the woodstove. He developed a system for cooking on the electric camp stove that involved turning the burner off and on at intervals to keep the frying pan from turning red hot. When I brought back Tupperware containers full of leftovers from our mother's kitchen, he would turn on that crazy stove and heat up the lot of it, dancing back and forth, left foot off, right foot on.

He addressed the squirrel problem every morning as soon as he woke up. He'd pull on his jeans and walk outside barefoot and shirtless carrying a shotgun, killing as many squirrels as he could before breakfast. He knew he would never substantially reduce the population in this way, but he figured that he would at least make life unpleasant for the squirrels who had claimed the house during the winter. In short order, the squirrels left us to build new nests in a safer environment.

In the backroom, he rigged up the bucket shower, the first warm water bathing apparatus ever installed in the old house. He bought a metal mop pail, and threaded a shower head and shut-off valve in a hole that he drilled in the bottom. He tied a rope to the handle of the bucket and ran it through a pulley system that he fastened to the ceiling in the old rain barrel shower stall. This allowed us to fill the bucket with warm water, pull it up above our heads, and then stand underneath it and open the valve to let gravity do its work.

His drive to improve the old house made me anxious. I didn't want to settle anywhere because doing so would mean I had left the past behind. I was so debilitated that I barely lifted a finger to help him. Even the most basic of household chores was impossible. Washing dishes required us to boil pots of water on one of the two makeshift stoves, filling a pan in the sink, and then rinsing in another pan. Most evening meals ended with dishes piled in the sink or, worse, stacked under chairs in the living room, where we would eat from our laps.

One day, I came home during a driving rainstorm to find that Walter had moved all of the dirty dishes into the yard to see if the rain would act as a kind of Mother Nature dishwasher. The dishes stayed outside in the yard for days until one of us, I can't recall who, boiled some water and cleaned up the mess.

My morning routine went something like this: I would hold the espresso maker while Walter operated the blowtorch. Once a cup of coffee was in hand, I filled a pot with water from the rain barrel and put it on the camp stove to boil. When the water reached showering temperature I filled the bucket and hoisted it to the ceiling. There was just enough water for a quick shampoo and rinse. Then I would carefully lift a suit and pressed shirt off the clothes rack, dress, and drive to my office, shaving in the car, having created what I hoped was a passable disguise of a successful and competent working man.

Once Walter had solved the coffee, showering, and squirrel problems, he tackled the next project on his priority list, which was to build a wood-fired sauna down by the shore. The house may have been falling apart around us, but for my brother, the sauna seemed to be the last convenience we would ever need, even if we decided to live at the old house for the rest of our lives, which at the time was as good a plan as any.

Walter was between jobs, waiting for an interview with the university for a full-time position in the recruiting office, so he had time on his hands. One morning, he drove to the lumberyard, filled his old white Chevy pickup with studs, and started framing up the sauna in a clearing beside the shore. When I came back in the evening, we would admire his progress and drink a couple beers, breathing the salt-drenched air and speaking softly of small matters as we watched the sky turn brilliant orange in the moments before the light lifted from the shore and the scene faded to black.

He framed up the sauna and we imagined ourselves swimming in the frigid waters of the bay and then dashing into the cedar-lined hut, where we would have long conversations and sweat away our troubles. Walter trucked in the tongue-and-groove cedar for the interior, a collection of short, irregular cast-offs from a local mill, which he stacked in the yard. We figured we were just weeks away from a good sweat.

Walter was and still is an excellent starter of projects, but in those days, he was a poor finisher. During the dark year, turning Walter onto a job was like pouring lighter fluid on wet charcoal. There is the immediate gratification of a big fire that holds lots of promise, and then the kerosene burns out and the coals smoulder and grow cold. Once Walter reached a certain point in a project, he was finished. He emotionally detached himself from the work and often never returned. The detachment hit him about the time he had the roof on the sauna. After he pounded the last nail, if someone had asked, "Hey, Walter, what are you doing tomorrow?"

he would have replied with a broad smile and said, "Nothing. Absolutely nothing."

For several days after he had the roof on the sauna, he rested. Then one evening I came home to find Walter sitting in a pile of rubble between the dining room and the kitchen, covered in dust, a sledge hammer resting on his knee. He had knocked down that unnecessary non-load-bearing wall and knocked it down good. This was another one of his excellent ideas. The kitchen and dining room were both small and cramped, and now we had a big country kitchen with plaster dust as far at the eye could see and electrical wires dangling from the ceiling. I have never seen a man as happy as Walter was at that moment. I shuddered, went upstairs, took off my suit, rolled into my crater, and tried to sleep. And so in this fashion, with Walter busy starting and not finishing, and me running full speed but not doing anything at all to change my circumstances, we proceeded through the summer.

Robert Pirsig would say that what was happening at the old house was the result of my brother's and my failing — for years — to do basic maintenance in our lives. Pirsig developed his famous motorcycle metaphor to illustrate how maintenance is as critical for a person's life as it is for the life of an internal combustion engine. "The place to improve the world is first in one's own heart and head and hands, and then work outward from there," Pirsig writes in *Zen and the Art of Motorcycle Maintenance*. "Other people can talk about how to expand the destiny of mankind. I just want to talk about how to fix a motorcycle." Self maintenance requires a slowing down so we can apply our full attention to the task at hand.

For Pirsig, there is a difference between good and bad maintenance. The key to good maintenance is caring. This requires that a person stop hurrying, something my brother and I had rarely done. "Zen Buddhists talk about 'just sitting,' a meditative practice in which the idea of a duality of self and object does not dominate one's consciousness," Pirsig writes. "What I'm talking about here in motorcycle maintenance is 'just fixing,' in which the idea of a duality of self and object doesn't dominate one's consciousness. When one is dominated by feelings of separateness from what he's working on, then one can be said to not 'care' about what he's doing. That is what caring really is, a feeling of identification with what one's doing."

Pirsig suggests that maintenance itself is an act of love, and that applies equally to maintenance of relationships with others and maintenance of the soul. "To live only for some future goal is shallow," he writes. "It's the sides of the mountain that sustain life, not the top."

I recall times when I was doing maintenance on my life, and caring for my family. This is not a state of being but a state of doing — of doing the little things that make a house a home. I have memories of stacking firewood outside the cottage on the shore of St. Margarets Bay, where we lived when I was a master's student, of working with my hands, sweating under my coat in the cool fall afternoon, the air filled with the smell of bark and split wood, my young daughter following me back and forth from the pile to the rows of firewood I was building by the back door, where they would be carried inside when the nights grew cold and winter snows began to fall.

Stacking wood requires the kind of caring that Pirsig describes, with each stick placed in its proper place in the row, where it will lie flat and true and support the row on top. If this job is done without proper care, the stacks collapse and the work has to begin again. I remember my neat stacks of wood outside that cottage, the sounds of my child's laughter in the clearing, and a time in my life when I was fully present in the small moments of the day.

But there are too many lost weeks and months in my past, when

I have only faint memories of day-to-day events. I was "half asleep," as Pirsig describes a procession of commuters he encounters on the highway at the beginning of his motorcycle journey with his son. I know that I lived for too many years in this state. Now at the old house, I was like Pirsig's commuters, hardly living at all. I was doing no maintenance, and Walter was starting jobs and not finishing them, which often made things worse than if the jobs had never been started at all.

That summer, Susan decided to visit us for a few weeks. She knew all about the guilt and fear. When she was a young woman, she fell in love at first sight and had a whirlwind romance. She and her boyfriend decided to get married, but by the time wedding plans were being made, she started having doubts that she was ready to be married. However, by then, she felt it was too late to back out. Once they were married, her doubts were confirmed, and she realized that her relationship had stopped her in her tracks. She felt that being one-half of a couple, somebody's wife, had caused her to disappear as a person. She thought she was a disappointment to her husband, and in the end, no amount of marriage counselling was going to fix this fundamental problem. She was the first of the siblings to be divorced — and for reasons that were difficult to explain to her family and friends.

When she came to the shore that summer, she started calling the old house the Betty Ford Clinic and decided that she would help make us more comfortable by finishing some of the renovations Walter had started. I came home one day to find her standing on a chair, her blonde hair tied up in a scarf, peeling off old wallpaper in the living room with a butter knife. Like her brothers, she had taken her lessons from my father's home improvement handbook. We convinced Susan to put down the butter knife, and then she was able to do what she does best, which is to love us up with good humour and good wine. For a time, the old house felt like a family home again, filled with laughter and fun. We stayed up late in the evenings talking about many things, including our difficulties in finding a way to make love and marriage work. None of us had any brilliant insights other than to acknowledge that, as hard as it was to be immersed in a crisis, it did present us with opportunities to change our lives if we were willing to take them. One evening when my brother and I were talking and pouring drinks in the living room and Susan was taking a minute to herself reading in her bedroom, Walter walked to the bottom of the stairs and called out, "Come downstairs, it's circle time." Susan stayed three weeks, and then we took her to the airport and drove back to the shore to fend for ourselves.

Although Walter was lost in an endless run of days, he did have one date on his calendar, the day of his job interview. One morning after I had left for work, the phone rang. Walter located it under a pile of debris on the dining-room floor. It was the interview panel calling. They were assembled and waiting for him; was he planning to come? He told them he thought the interview was on the seventh of the month. "It is the seventh," the caller replied. There was a long pause. Could he do the interview by phone? "Certainly," Walter replied. He asked for a moment to get settled in his home office. He held his hand over the receiver and with his other arm swept the layers of debris from the destroyed wall off the dining-room table onto the floor. He picked the phone off the floor and placed it in the cleared area on the table, waved the dust out of the air, composed himself, and started answering questions. Somehow, he landed the job. We laughed till we cried when he retold the story, and that night we celebrated new beginnings, a tentative step for one of us into new territory.

12

I recognized that while Walter was moving forward, I was stuck and needed help dislodging myself. So I made an appointment to see Kersti Covert, a psychiatrist in Saint John. On a misty summer afternoon, I walked from my newspaper office to her second-floor office in an old brick building on the waterfront. I sat in the waiting room listening to the classical music station on the radio in the corner. In time, I would come to rely on her running late and bring work with me, but during this first visit, I waited alone, reading outdated issues of *People* magazine and slipping outside from time to time to smoke in the doorway.

Finally, her office door opened and she invited me in. The windows looked out on the cargo sheds, longshoreman's lunch-rooms, and flat grey water of the harbour. The walls were crowded with art and the tables were piled high with a jumble of books. Dr. Covert is plump, blond, brilliant, and never in a hurry, which explains why she so often runs behind schedule. A session often begins with her monologue about the chaotic state of her life, which I eventually came to understand was her way of helping me to relax. When I was becoming completely absorbed by the story of her weekly personal and professional crises, she would start asking questions: So what's going on with you? You looked really stressed when you came in. Now you look better. Tell me what's going on?

Then she would wait for me to start talking. I began that first session by telling her about Deb and how I had thought I was doing the right thing by levelling with my wife, but now my life and the lives of my wife and children were in disarray. This had been my comfortable narrative; it was almost a set piece by then. I was an honest man who had been honest with his wife. I hadn't had an extramarital affair, and now I was suffering the consequences of being honest. Dr. Covert took notes and looked at me from time to time with what I thought was sympathy until I told her for the second or third time about how badly I felt about how I had hurt my former wife.

"So what?" she interjected, stopping my soliloquy in its tracks. "She's an attractive woman. I'm sure she'll find someone better." She looked down at her notes, then back at me, and waited for a response. I laughed nervously, thinking she had made a joke, but then I realized she wasn't laughing.

Now that she had my full attention, she started to lay the groundwork for how we would work together. She told me that although we make a marriage vow to be faithful to our spouse, humans are not made to be monogamous. Which is a good thing, because if we lose our spouse, we may fall in love again and have another chance at a happy partnership with someone else. So it is a good thing that we can fall in love with more than one person in a lifetime, and a bad thing, because we say our marriage vows and we want to live up to them, and many of us want to be faithful, but then our circumstances change. When we fall in love with someone, we have positive feelings for that person. When these feelings disappear, it's hard to find them again. Sometimes we can recover these positive feelings, sometimes we can't. Sometimes one partner has outgrown the other, and as a couple, they simply don't fit any more.

She smiled and told me that her husband always maintained that getting a divorce is a waste of time because we just trade one set of problems for another. Marriage is always a challenge. We have needs that marriage sometimes fills and sometimes frustrates, and there are no guarantees. We may fall in love, but we should never presume that we can fall into a successful marriage.

Anyone who leaves a marriage experiences grief, she said, and this grief is often accompanied by guilt. She noted that I was obviously consumed by both. No matter how badly we may want to end a relationship, we still grieve for what we have lost because in the beginning it wasn't all bad. In fact, it may have been very good. We may share children and many other profound connections

51

that need to be either severed or reconstructed before we are able to begin building a loving relationship with someone else. She said she might be able help me with this task.

Dr. Covert told me that if I were to try to make a life with Deb, there was a good chance our relationship wouldn't last — unless I was willing to do the work I needed to do to grow and mature and achieve something greater and better than I had at that moment. At the end of that process, Deb might be there for me, or she might not.

When we leave a relationship that is not working, we need to lay that relationship to rest, she said. Only then can we find a new partner and get to know that person in his or her own right, and not as a piece that's missing from the first relationship. We have to use our heads and our hearts, she told me. It's not all heart. Falling in love is not enough. Love is not enough. We can fall in love many times, but the person we choose has to be someone we think we can share things with, someone we can live with, someone we admire and respect. Falling in love may be mysterious and powerful and exciting, but making love last requires a union of the head and the heart.

So, she asked, did I want to work with her? I mumbled yes, and then suddenly, the session was over. I staggered out into the misty afternoon, walked slowly back to the newspaper office, put my head into the news of the day long enough to get my newspaper out on the street, and then drove to the old house, where I lay awake most of the night replaying my conversation with Dr. Covert in my tired mind.

13

That summer, Deb and I were reading a book at work called *News Is a Verb*, written by New York newspaper editor and columnist Pete Hamill. In his lament for the state of journalism at the turn of this century, Hamill argues that writing the news, telling the stories of our community, demands that we be more than just passive stenographers at institutional press conferences, allowing others to set the agenda for a profession that is supposed to embrace freedom of expression and creative thinking.

News isn't something we seek, some object that we uncover, polish, and transfer into the pages of a newspaper. News is something that emerges from our own active participation in the life of the communities where we live and work. We don't happen upon the news; we make news happen by living each day with our eyes open to the world. Deb told me that she had been reading Hamill's book and thinking about the nature of love.

"You know, love is a verb," she said, keeping her eyes fixed on mine long enough to make sure I understood she was talking about us. And so over time, we began talking and thinking about the nature of love, that mysterious movement of hearts and minds that defines us as humans.

Years after that first conversation about love as a verb, I have come to the conclusion that the proper response to "I love you," uttered for the first time, is not "I love you too" but something like "That's really nice, now what are you going to do about it?"

British literary critic Terry Eagleton writes in *The Meaning of Life*, his concise book of big ideas, that love is the way in which we reconcile our desire for individual fulfillment with the fact that we are social animals who seek out associations with others. "For love means creating for another the space in which he might flourish, at the same time as he does this for you," Eagleton writes. "The fulfilment of each becomes the ground for the fulfilment of the other. When we realize our natures in this way, we are at our best." This is a love that offers us the opportunity to be all we can be in this world.

The love we strive for in adult partnerships is different from the powerful, unconditional love we feel immediately for our children. "One may love one's small infants to the point of being cheerfully prepared to die for them; but because loving in the fullest sense is something the infants themselves are going to have to learn, the love between you and them cannot be the prototype of human love, any more than can a less precious relationship like one's affection for a loyal old butler," Eagleton writes. "In both cases, the relationship is not equal enough." Love, in the fullest, active sense of the word, is a relationship between equals that allows for the "the fullest possible reciprocity." The love between equals is not unconditional; the condition is reciprocity. Love is a verb.

The English language is confusing because the word *love* is tossed about casually and interchangeably. We say "I love you" and we say "I love black olives on my pizza." The ancient Greeks recognized different types of love in their language by having different words for them. The Greek word *eros* is perhaps best translated as desire or erotic love. When we fall in love, we are consumed by *eros*. "Human sex is inseparable from the activity of the imagination," writes Allan Bloom in *Love and Friendship*, his reflection on the nature of *eros*. "Everybody knows this. The body's secret movements are ignited by some images and turned off by others. Ideas of beauty and merit, as well as longings for eternity, are first expressed in the base coin of bodily movements."

Poet and Greek scholar Anne Carson writes in her eloquent and intriguing exploration of *eros* and the work of the poet Sappho: "The Greek word *eros* denotes 'want,' 'lack,' 'desire for what is missing.' The lover wants what he does not have." Carson's writing about the nature of *eros* begins with a fragment of Sappho in which the poet describes *eros* as *glukupikron*, or "sweetbitter." She observes that Sappho recognized the contradiction in *eros* and the inherent risk and the irresistible nature of desire. "Eros is always a story in which lover, beloved and the difference between them interact," Carson writes. "The interaction is a fiction arranged by the mind of the lover. It carries an emotional charge both hateful and delicious and emits a light like knowledge."

The Greek word *philia* is another kind of love that we translate as "friendship," a form of human interaction that Aristotle held in the highest regard and that he describes as a relationship among equals, in which we rejoice in each other's achievements and give in kind. "Aristotle stretches the definition of friendship considerably to mean sharing, life together, communion," writes Jean Vanier in *Made for Happiness*, his commentary on the *Nichomachean Ethics*. "Nothing pushes us quite as radically beyond ourselves as friendship." Vanier notes that while erotic love feeds on fantasy and uncertainty, in true friendship we are more secure and less troubled. "Friendship is primarily a life together that is nourished by shared activity and not by dreams about another person."

The Greek word *agape* is less translatable but connotes love in its most universal form, the essence of humanity at its best, expressed when we reach out to each other in times of need. *Agape* "has nothing to do with erotic or even affectionate feelings," Eagleton writes. "The command to love is purely impersonal: the prototype of it is loving strangers, not those you desire or admire. It is a practice or way of life, not a state of mind."

We seek these various kinds of love in marriage; we seek desire and erotic love; friendship; and the opportunity to be all we can be, the best we can be, as humans. This idea of love holds the greatest possibilities for us in this life. But if we seek all of this in a relationship with a single other person, we set out enormously high expectations from the beginning. Even if we find this all-encompassing love for a time, preserving it during a lifetime is no small matter.

14

Late one afternoon near the end of one of my sessions with Dr. Covert, I was telling her about my routine of waking up at dawn, driving forty-five minutes to the farm on mornings when my former wife was working, getting breakfast for the kids and helping them get ready for school, then driving another thirty minutes to my office and working all day. "Why are you doing this?" she asked.

"Because my kids need me there," I replied. Well, I qualified this. My daughters could look after things. In fact, they were both graduates of a babysitting course and knew the morning routine as well as I did. But Aaron was only nine. He needed me in the mornings. What would happen when the weather got colder and he forgot to wear his mittens?

"He'll remember to wear his mittens," Dr. Covert said, "especially if he doesn't wear them one day and his hands get really cold. It sounds to me like this routine is something you need to do." Then she said, "That's fine that you need this, but don't justify it by saying the kids need you. You need this, or you don't need this. It's as simple as that."

It was a good thing for me to be there for my children, but I needed to understand that I was there because I wanted to be, not because they needed me so desperately. I needed to start doing what I wanted to do with my life, and to stop walking through my days as if I had no control of my own agenda. I needed to start making decisions, both large and small.

I sat in my chair wrestling with this and then asked the one question that I never should have asked.

"I don't know what to do. What do you think I should do?"

She looked at me for a moment and then replied, "Don't ask me, I'm not your momma."

Men often become childlike in a marriage, she said. We tell our friends that we would love to come out and play but that "the old lady" won't let us. Or we let "the old lady" do our laundry and cook our meals while we go out and play with our friends. Or we go on trips with the "boys" and drink too much and chase women and then come back home and tell lies about the nature of the trip.

We should not live our lives in spite of our wives. We shouldn't ask the women in our lives for permission to live how we want to live. Women need equal partners; they do not need another child underfoot. I was behaving like a child, acting as if I were a victim of circumstances beyond my control, and looking for someone to tell me what to do. Dr. Covert was telling me to grow up and recognize that I had the freedom to make choices that were good for me, and good for the people I loved.

Early in my career as a reporter, one of my editors told me that the life of a journalist didn't offer much in the way of job security or working conditions or financial compensation, but that it did offer freedom. That freedom came in the opportunity to tell the stories we wanted to tell and to tell them how we saw them. I had found this freedom in my work, and over the years I had exercised this freedom in the telling of other people's stories. Now I needed to acknowledge that I had the freedom to design my own life story.

Dr. Covert's approach always returned the responsibility for change back to me. However, accepting the responsibility in her office and exercising it were two different things. Love is a verb, and living a life of love required me to exercise my freedom, take action, and make some choices.

I was reminded of this one afternoon late in the first summer of the dark year when Deb called me at the old house to tell me she had spent the day with a friend at a beach nearby and that they were at a local restaurant. She asked me to drive over and join them for a beer on the patio. Deb was sitting in a chair ordering food when I arrived, her hair pulled back, her face flushed from a day spent in the sun. I stopped in the doorway of the restaurant, consumed with a terrible combination of longing and anxiety. When I walked over, she recognized the anxiety in my expression. She continued to watch me with sadness in her eyes as I drank my beer and tried to make conversation. Before I left, Deb explained that she was patient, but that at some point she needed to move on with her life, with me, or without me in it. I left the restaurant alone and drove slowly back to the old house.

15

In the weeks that followed, I decided that I needed to do something about my living conditions. Once I was standing on my own two feet, perhaps I could begin to involve another person in my life. To begin the process, my brother and I needed to start doing some maintenance. On a Saturday morning early in the fall of the dark year, Walter and I started cleaning up. Both the kitchen and dining room were still under construction. The living room was filled with furniture from the dining room. There was no place to sit. If I wanted to talk on the phone, I had to untangle the cord and drag it out onto the front porch and sit on the steps. The front parlour room was filled with piles of Walter's unpacked junk and garbage bags filled with my books.

We worked through Walter's piles first, throwing most of the stuff away, and then unpacked my books. We started on the living room and kitchen, sweeping up debris, washing dishes, and taking stock of what we needed to make a real home. We walked down to the beach and found a long driftwood pole, strapped a television antenna to the top, and fastened it to the side of the house in the back. We ran a wire inside and hooked it up to an old black-and-white television we found in the upstairs closet so we could watch hockey games on Saturday nights. About noon, I telephoned my children and told them I would see them on Sunday instead of Saturday because I needed a day to get my house in order.

We moved through the house bagging up garbage and junk and sweeping the corners. We pulled sheets of linoleum off the floors to expose weathered softwood boards. We opened the closet at the top of the stairs and started sorting through decades-old camping equipment and toys. I even changed the sheets on my crater bed.

Late in the afternoon, we loaded the refrigerator, which was small and barely functioning, onto the back of Walter's truck and drove down the highway to the now vacant farmhouse where he had been living with his former wife. We exchanged the fridge for a larger, newer model he had purchased months ago but never retrieved. We loaded the fridge and a couch on the back of the truck, along with some other possessions he had left behind. He had been putting off this final trip to the house for too long. We started back just as the sun set and the rain started. The couch cushions blew onto the highway and we had to turn back and find them in the dark, but nothing could discourage us that day.

We fell into bed late that night, exhausted. When I awoke the next morning and made breakfast and prepared to spend the day with my children, I felt very alone. And being alone felt just fine. My brother and I had taken a small step forward together. We were beginning to make a home for ourselves, and for my children.

16

Throughout the fall, we left all the windows open. We wanted to hear the waves, to feel the comforting pulse of the shore, day and night. The windows stayed open even when it rained, even when the nights started getting colder and we had to throw more blankets on our beds. It wasn't until the chilling rains of late October blew in off the bay that we reluctantly pulled the windows shut. We immediately felt isolated in our home out on McPherson's Point.

A few weeks later, the grey skies started spitting wet snow. The north winds drove the waves onto the beach, the stones and seaweed were coated in ice, and we were slipping and sliding on the front porch as we replaced storm windows and doors and tried to remember why we had decided to spend the winter in this place, especially when we hadn't finished building our sauna and had no indoor toilet, no source of heat other than the old cookstove in the kitchen, not even any insulation in the walls. Walter was in the process of installing a conventional indoor shower and hot-water tank in a closet off the kitchen, but in the meantime we were shivering under the languid flow of the bucket shower in the frosty mornings before we left for work.

We needed to find a source of heat for the old house or we needed to find a new place to live. It may have been more practical for us to find a warmer place for the winter. I think we decided to stay because we knew we needed each other, although we may not have admitted it at the time. Chance may have brought us together, but even on days when my brother and I were driving each other crazy, we still showed each other love in all kinds of ways. We listened to each other talk without passing judgment or offering unsolicited advice. We picked up two beers from the fridge during Saturday-night hockey games, made coffee for each other in the mornings, and occasionally brought in food so we could share a meal. Even on nights when we were incapable of doing much more than rolling exhausted into bed, we'd always say, "I love you, brother" before we did.

Finally, when we could no longer ignore the coming of winter, my brother, the fixer, came up with a plan to heat the house with firewood, borrowed a used woodstove from our father's garage, and installed it in the living room. As we fed wood into the stove and braced ourselves for the darkest months of the dark year, I added another decision to my series of bad decisions. I decided that I needed a better vehicle than the slightly battered but reliable Volkswagen Jetta I was driving, something that would transport me and my children safely through the snow and ice. So I traded my car for a used, full-sized, red-and-white Ford F150 four-wheel drive with an extended cab, a fibreglass cap, and a V8 engine that burned so much gas it needed both its gas tanks to get me from one gas station to the next. It had a button on the dash that allowed me to switch to tank number two when tank number one went dry, which happened with alarming regularity.

I remember only one occasion when the truck proved useful. When the pond beside the far beach froze and my children were staying with us for the weekend, we decided to go skating. I had learned to skate on that pond. My mother and father were brave souls from warmer climates who knew nothing about winter sports but were determined that we would all learn to skate and ski like real Canadians. It might have been easier for us to learn to skate in one of the indoor rinks in town, but that would have stripped all the Presbyterian fun out of it. On winter weekends, we would drive to the shore, where my father would light a fire beside the pond and we would sit on cold logs, tie on our skates with frozen fingers, and take to the ice.

We would drag along kitchen chairs for support as we slipped and staggered across the ice. As novice skaters, we would spend the morning scraping across the pond, with most of our energy going into falling, and weeping, and pulling ourselves back up on the chairs. The one blessing in all of this was that the old house is situated at the end of a long dead end and no one had to witness this lurching scene. One Saturday, my father fell so hard on his head that the apple-sized lump on his forehead turned into a black eye. That Sunday morning, he followed the choir into the church with a deep purple shiner and a grim smile.

I never learned to skate and play hockey as well as my Canadian-born friends, but the next generation did. My girls took skating lessons and learned to skate really well soon after they could walk. Aaron had been playing organized hockey since he was in kindergarten and had grown into a fine forward who knew how to put the puck in the net. The girls took up hockey when a women's league started in our neighbourhood and were both solid players, particularly Danielle, who was small in stature but fast. Gabby wasn't as fast a skater as Danielle, but she was rock solid on her feet and liked to go into the corners with a crowd of players and come out with the puck. During the dark year, the girls were both on the same line on their hockey team, Danielle swirling around on right wing, Gabrielle grinding it out on left, and their dad pacing along the bleachers with a big happy smile on his face.

So when the pond froze, my children and I made plans to go skating. I bought skate guards, and the kids tied on their skates by the woodstove in the house. Then we climbed into my new truck, and I shifted into four-wheel drive and drove us down across the creek to the edge of the pond.

I sat on the tailgate and tied on my skates and we spent a glorious day skating and playing pickup hockey. Walter came down and joined the game with his usual reckless abandon, playing so hard that he eventually collapsed on the ice and rested while the kids skated circles around him, poking him with their sticks, mocking him for growing old and not keeping up. That day, our troubles were consumed by the game, which continued for hours under the early winter sun.

When I am playing pond hockey, I can understand why the ancient Greeks believed that games imitate the life of the gods, for a game is complete in itself, has no end outside of itself. Therefore, we best express our freedom in games, especially in games like pond hockey when no one is keeping score. We find a temporary respite from the necessities of day-to-day living; games are an essential part of performing maintenance on our souls. Robert Pirsig would have approved. I remember feeling such tremendous relief out there on the ice that day. I could feel it in all of us.

17

In December, my father's mother, whom we called Gan-Gan, died at the age of ninety-five. She had outlived Pa by seven years, and though she grew weak and deaf in the final years of her life, she remained mentally sharp and maintained her sweet nature right to the end. We flew to Florida to attend her funeral at the neighbourhood Presbyterian church that she and her husband had attended for most of their adult lives. My father robed and participated in the service, as he had done when his father died. These services must have been terribly difficult for him, but he appeared to be filled by a kind of quiet grace and gratitude that he was able to help us all lay Gan-Gan to rest. She was buried beside her husband, and after a brief graveside prayer service, we gathered in my grandparents' home for a meal, all feeling the ache of the loss.

My grandmother was a tiny, delicate woman, standing five feet tall in her shoes, a frame both my sisters inherited. She had impeccable manners that, for those who didn't know her, disguised her remarkably strong will. She would always respond to anything I said as a child with her favourite expression, "Well I declare." My grandparents had survived Pa's years of travelling and working obsessively for the railroad and had grown old together. Pa had imagined that he and his wife would stay at the old house during their summer visits to Canada, but in the end a house with no indoor plumbing was too rough for my grandmother. She needed her hot bath in the evenings, so they would stay at my parents' house in town and drive out to the shore to be with us during the day.

For two days after the funeral, my brother and sisters and I stayed together at a bachelor beach condominium my grandparents owned near St. Petersburg. It had been years since we were all together. My older sister, Sadie, who had lived near me and was my best friend when I was studying in Nova Scotia, had moved to Nashville, Tennessee, where she was married and raising two children, deep in the midst of her worrisome years.

The days on the Florida beach felt out of time and place, with Christmas decorations going up and carols being played in the shopping malls and restaurants. We drank cases of chilled Mexican Corona beer with lime slices pushed into the tops of the bottles and ate Cuban sandwiches and grilled fish and marked as best we could the passing of our grandmother, who had been a constant presence in our lives, even when she lived so far away. We swam in the Gulf of Mexico and soaked up the warmth of the sun. The greatest gift my parents gave to their children was our connection with one another, and I told myself during those days at the beach that I wanted to do everything I could to pass that gift on to my children.

When Walter and I landed at the airport in Saint John, we pulled our winter coats, hats, and gloves out of our suitcases and drove straight to the beer store. We bought a case of Corona and stopped at the grocery store for limes, hoping to rekindle some of the warmth we had found on the beach. When we arrived at the old house, we shovelled the snow away from the back door, brought in armloads of wood, and lit a fire in the stove. We cracked open the beer, found a knife to slice a lime, and huddled together, shivering in our coats. We choked down one beer each and then mumbled that it was time to go to bed. The case of Corona went into the fridge and stayed there till spring.

The wood we had put in for the winter ran out early in the new year. We made desperate phone calls to wood suppliers, who wished us good luck when we asked if they could deliver us a load of dry firewood in January. Finally, just when we were about to start breaking up the furniture to feed the stove, Walter found a man who promised to deliver us a load of wood, although there were no guarantees about how dry it would be. One evening, we arrived home to find a load of split hardwood dumped by the back door.

We eventually decided that this wood must have been excavated from the bottom of a swamp. The sticks were waterlogged, coated in ice and gravel, and simply would not burn. Many nights I came home from work and after spending an hour trying and failing to get a fire started, I would give up, go upstairs, and put on more clothes before burrowing into my crater under piles of blankets and shivering through the night.

One evening, I happened on a secret stash of cedar kindling that Walter had hidden away behind the kitchen cookstove for use in emergencies. I unilaterally declared a state of emergency and lit a lovely fire. I fed in one stick after another, warming myself in the flames and scrambling a pan of eggs for supper, boiling the kettle to make tea. I was having Little Match Girl hallucinations when Walter arrived home and realized that I was burning his stash.

He began to frantically gather the remaining sticks that were scattered around the stove, all the while shouting that I was threatening our very survival in the house; we would freeze to death if we could never light another fire in the stove after my little indulgence. I took my eggs and tea off the stove and sat at the kitchen table and told him between mouthfuls of eggs and slugs of hot tea that I didn't care about his stupid kindling because he was the one who bought us the ridiculous swampwood and no amount of dry kindling would solve that problem.

In hindsight, I realize we were both right, but for the first time since we had been at the old house together, we almost came to blows. The problem wasn't the wood or the cold. The problem was that although we had made the shell of a home out of the chaos of our lives, we were both still stuck and not really living at all. At that point we knew we were locked into a holding pattern for the rest of the winter. Somehow we held it together. I started hauling loads of kindling back to the house in my truck that helped us light fires with the swampwood, which eventually started to dry, and carry on through the final hard months of winter.

18

Winters in Atlantic Canada last about two months too long. By March we are ready for spring and always think we are nearing the end when, in fact, the worst is often yet to come. One March evening when I was driving home through freezing rain, I noticed several cars ahead of me had gone off the road. I was driving my big rig in four-wheel drive and felt safe, but I decided I'd better pull over to find out just how slippery the conditions had become. When I stepped out onto the road, I found it covered with an invisible sheet of wet ice that was so slippery I could barely keep my footing as I inched my way back to the truck. I considered my options. Within minutes, a police cruiser with lights flashing came crawling down the highway, ordering all traffic off the road until the highway could be salted and sanded. Then word filtered down from car to car that the salt truck had slid into a ditch. So I stayed on the side of the road most of the night, catnapping and reading old newspapers I found on the floor of the truck, hungry and thirsty because I had skipped dinner in the rush of work deadlines, and running the heat as little as possible to preserve gas, which wasn't easy in the big Ford.

I had lots of time to think that night. I was wishing I was anywhere but there, and I was wishing for the end of winter and the dark year. I knew I needed to find a way to leave the old house and begin to construct a real life in a home of my own. When the salt truck finally came by in the early morning, I pulled carefully back onto the highway and made it to the old house. After a few hours of sleep, I drove back to the newspaper office. While I was sleeping, the temperature had risen and the ice had melted off the road and it was clear sailing, as if the night before had never happened. No one at the office had heard about the cars trapped on the highway all night, and I worried for a time that maybe I had dreamed the whole episode and that perhaps I was finally losing my mind.

So much was coming at me at once. I was worried about the consequences of separating myself financially from my wife, the anticipated final division of our assets. And there were unanswered questions about where we would all live in the long term and what kind of permanent arrangements we would make about parenting our children. Decisions had to be made. The only certainty was that something had to change.

In April, the winter finally broke. My brother and I had survived with our love for each other and all our parts intact. In May, the warm breezes came to the shore, the grass turned green, and the wildflowers bloomed in the field. For a time, Walter and I discussed the possibility of renovating the old house and continuing to live there together on a more permanent basis. The Bay of Fundy shore has a way of seducing people. After the first warm day of sitting on the porch in lawn chairs, with the rediscovered case of Corona beside us, we forgot about the cold runs to the outhouse, the swampwood, and the unfortunate kindling incident, and decided there was no place on earth we would rather be. I even went so far as to have a contractor give us a quote on building a small addition on the house so I could live there with the children when they came.

About the time these discussions got serious, Walter and I started arguing in a way that we never had during the dark year. Walter had fallen for a woman with a three-year-old son, and he thought that in the future he might want to have them living at the old house too. We argued about how this would all work, and then said we were sorry, and I realized that I was fantasizing about a living arrangement that could never work. I needed to make plans to leave the old house before fall.

First, I had to get my finances in order. Nashville songwriter Todd Snider wrote an ode to prenuptial agreements called "Just in Case" that includes the truism "Well you know I can't love you enough, but I also can't afford to lose half of my stuff." Under Canada's no-fault divorce law, each party receives half of everything.

It's a split down the middle in theory, but the division is almost always more complicated than that. In the beginning, I wanted to give everything away — a decision driven by guilt. I had failed as a husband and therefore would pay for my shortcomings with money and possessions. My lawyer told me that I would need to hire someone else to prepare a deal like that. She told me that giving away the farm, in my case literally, is a mistake men commonly make. She convinced me to take a few weeks to consider that my responsibility to my children required that I stay financially afloat.

In the end, I did stay afloat, but barely. In time, I decided that a divorce can have a wonderfully liberating effect on a person's worries about money. When a man is approaching forty and has nothing to his name but a mountain of debt, money seems to matter less. Late in that second summer, I separated my finances from my former wife's, and for many years after the dark year, financial management for me was simply managing my debt. I learned to say the words "it's only money" and mean it. Before I could move forward and try to make a life with someone else, I wanted to know that I could survive and be happy living alone.

19

Love is a verb. Saying it is easy. Living it is difficult, but perhaps that's the point. Homer, the greatest of the Greek poets, makes this clear in his *Odyssey*, when we find the hero shipwrecked on an island with the goddess Kalypso, who desires him for a husband. She feeds him fresh island-grown food and fine wine and takes him to bed every night and makes passionate love to him, as only a goddess can. She promises him immortality if he will stay with her. However, the poet tells us that every day Odysseus sits alone by the edge of the sea and weeps, contemplating suicide. He wants to return home to Ithaca and his wife, Penelope.

He has been away for twenty years, ten years fighting the war at Troy and ten years wandering the seas on his long journey home. Why does Odysseus want to return home? Home is not only the physical island of Ithaca, but also a spiritual destination. He is not a god, and he would risk everything, including his own life, rather than lose himself in the arms of a goddess. Kalypso is not offering him a chance at love. There is no reciprocity in her island world.

When Kalypso asks Odysseus what it is about Penelope that makes her so special, he asks the goddess not to be angry with him, that it is not some adolescent crush that has left him weeping on the shore looking out at the sea and longing for a homecoming.

> *Look at my wise Penelope. She falls far short of you,*
> *your beauty, stature. She is mortal after all*
> *and you, you never age or die . . .*
> *Nevertheless I long — I pine all my days —*
> *to travel home and see the dawn of my return.*
> *And if a god will wreck me yet again on the wine-dark sea,*
> *I can bear that too, with a spirit tempered to endure.*
> *Much have I suffered, labored long and hard by now*
> *in the waves and wars. Add this to the total —*
> *bring the trial on!*

Homer's modern audience is often taken aback that the hero doesn't tell the goddess that he loves Penelope. But of course he can't possibly love her from such a great distance. Instead he says, Bring the trial on. This is what makes the poem an enduring love story and not some dime-store romance. He wants to go home and he is willing to throw himself at the mercy of the turbulent seas to get there. Odysseus wants to live, and he wants to love, and for Homer's hero, for all of us, living and loving is not an invitation to paradise.

All of us long for a homecoming, to arrive at a place where we can be all we can be. It took me many years to understand that this thing we called home is not a place on this earth but a place of the mind and imagination where we can find love, friendship, and freedom. George Dimock, one of the great translators and interpreters of *The Odyssey*, notes that only when Odysseus has declared his independence from the goddess does she call him by his full name, "Zeus-spring son of Laertes, ingenious Odysseus," which in the Greek is a complete hexameter line of epithets. "When Odysseus answers that, less beautiful though Penelope may be, he would still like to go home and see the day of his return; that, even if some god should wreck him on the sea, he can stand that too; war and the waves he has often known; this would only be more of the same — when he replies in this way, he seems very fine," Dimock writes.

"Odysseus, we may feel, was made, and so is any mortal, to fight and struggle and come home at last; not to be eternally safe and satisfied and free of ills. If this is what was in Homer's mind, Odysseus returns to Penelope because that way he can best fulfill himself as a man — that is the basis of his faithfulness . . . Odysseus was 'the man,' according to the [poem's] invocation, who experienced and suffered so much 'in the struggle to save his life and bring his comrades home.' Now we see that 'saving one's life' is more than a matter of physical survival. Kalypso offered an eternity of that. Is it too much to say that what Odysseus is saving and has had to save from her is his integrity, his identity?" Odysseus longed to return to Ithaca, because that was the place where he could be Odysseus. That's what a homecoming is about.

In Homer's world, divine intervention is needed to release Odysseus from the island. The divine intervention works as it always does with the Greeks, in concert with human action. The goddess Athena informs Kalypso that Odysseus is destined to return home, that his return has been sanctioned by Zeus. Kalypso reluctantly tells her lover that he is free to go. Then Odysseus takes matters into his own hands. "Gods may bask at ease; mortals must have something to do," writes Dimock. "Odysseus builds a boat, the boat which means that he is rejoining the mortal world, and for this reason every detail of its construction becomes more interesting. How refreshing after seven years of inactivity is all this cutting and doweling and fitting! Human art and skill, useless in Kalypso's paradise, now come into their own. Tools 'fit the hand,' and all is done 'expertly.' And now it makes sense to count the days."

It was the fourth day, and he had everything finished.
The fifth came, and Kalypso sent him off from her island.

"Time matters now! And so, 'In joy Odysseus set his sail to the following wind.' "

The story of my life was no Greek epic, to be sure, and I had not washed up on an island to be loved by a goddess. But at the old house by the sea I was stranded on an island of sorts. Dimock tells us that the name Kalypso is related to a verb that means to shroud or hide. On the island, Odysseus was being Kalypsoed, hidden from the world in a place where he was denied freedom and love. In that sense, the old house was my hiding place. I had Kalypsoed myself there.

It was time for me to bring on the trial. This, of course, is what living and loving is. We take matters into our own hands, make deliberate choices, and accept the risks of setting out across the dangerous seas.

20

That spring, Deb took a new job and moved an hour's drive north, to the city of Fredericton. During the dark year, we had continued to work together for a time. Then there had been a management shuffle in the head office of the company that owned my newspaper that included a new editorial director, and I decided to leave my editor's role to become a writer for the paper. I was on the road pursuing stories, or writing at home, and rarely came to the office. We saw each other infrequently. Deb's move to Fredericton was a decision she made to get on with her life while I sorted out the mess of mine with my brother at the old house.

She needed help on moving day and had asked me if I could lend her a hand when the truck arrived at her new apartment. I told her that I couldn't commit to being there, that I didn't know what would be happening that day. This kind of vague response to a specific request was typical of my paralysis during the dark year. Deb wasn't asking me to promise my life to her. She just needed a friend with a strong back to move some boxes, and I was being profoundly unhelpful. So she did what any reasonable person would do: she disconnected her phone and moved without giving me her new address.

Her moving day arrived and I woke up alone in my crater bed at the old house remembering that love is a verb. I drove to Fredericton to search for her, knowing only that she was moving somewhere downtown on the south side of the St. John River. After an hour of driving aimlessly about, I finally reached her on her cell phone, which she had turned on to call a hardware store. I asked her for forgiveness and directions to her new apartment. She paused, then reluctantly gave me the address. She told me she was on the way to the hardware store to buy a saw to cut her double-bed box spring in half because it wouldn't fit up the narrow staircase to her new bedroom.

I found her in the apartment with the saw in her hand, preparing to create a single bed, because, she assured me, that was the only kind of bed she would need for quite some time. She was surrounded by boxes, disillusioned and angry with me. I spent the day sawing the bed and helping her set up her new apartment. I redeemed myself for a few hours on that day, but our long-term prospects were not looking good.

Weeks later, we discussed the possibility of taking a vacation together. I knew it was time to push off from my island. So we made plans to get out of town. One morning in late summer, I packed up the big rig and left Walter to mind the old house for a couple of weeks. About a block from Deb's apartment, I blew out one of the front tires. I found that I had worn the tires right through. I had never slowed down to do even the most basic maintenance on the truck, or even to glance at the state of my tires. I was reminded again of just how reckless and out of control my life had become during the dark year.

I wrestled a jack under the truck, put on a spare tire, and drove to a service station where I had two used tires installed on the front rims. When I finally arrived to pick up Deb, shaken and covered with grease and dirt, we drove cautiously down the highway toward Halifax, where we had plans to visit Deb's family and, if possible, get rid of the Ford forever.

At a dealership in Halifax, I traded the truck for a small, used Toyota SUV, discovering that by some miracle my credit was still good enough to negotiate a car loan. We visited with Deb's parents and then drove to northern New Brunswick to a beach cottage owned by a newspaper columnist and long-time friend who had offered to loan us the place for as long as we needed it.

We arrived at the cottage late in the afternoon and found our friend standing on the back porch. The main cottage is a ramshackle red and white Cape Cod with a screened porch built on pilings beside Youghall Beach, a long stretch of white sand and dunes beside the Bay of Chaleur. The little two-bedroom cottage we were using is set back on the other side of a dirt road. When we arrived, we found the lot overrun with our friend's grandchildren and their friends, preteens and young teens. The children had built a bonfire on the beach in front of the cottage and invited us down to roast marshmallows and howl at the moon.

We traipsed around the fire until the children started to get tired and went in search for places to sleep. We stumbled off to our cabin. The next morning, when we took our coffee out onto the front steps of our cabin, we watched sleepy-eyed children emerge from the cottage and from the back seats of cars in the driveway, still wearing the bathing suits they would wear all week.

For ten days we played with the children on the beach, took long walks, and swam in the warm waters of the bay. Each day we slowed down the pace of our lives. We bought groceries and good bottles of wine; cooked meals together; lingered over breakfast, lunch, and dinner. We carried our folding chairs to the beach and sat on the sand flats and read books to each other, moving our chairs up and down the shore with the changing of the tides.

One of the books we read was Anne Michaels's *Fugitive Pieces*, a novel that tells the story of Jacob Beer, a poet and Polish Jew, who as a boy survives by hiding in the mud while Nazi soldiers kill his family. He is rescued by a Greek scientist who takes the boy to the island of Zakynthos and hides him there until the end of the occupation. After the war, Jacob travels to Toronto, where he learns to translate poetry and in the process learns to make the choices he needs to find happiness in his life. "You can choose your philosophy of translation just as you choose how to live: the free adaptation that sacrifices detail to meaning, the strict crib that sacrifices meaning to exactitude," he says. "The poet moves from life to language, the translator moves from language to life."

Jacob marries in Toronto, is divorced, and returns to Greece to try to restart his life. He finds a great and passionate love with his second wife, Michaela, whom meets during a visit to Toronto. Anne Michaels writes of an image in one of Jacob's poems, about an impossibly high wall and a man standing on each side, each man trying to decide if and how they might pass over it. In this life, some will strive to pass over the walls that rise up before us, and some will not. "Some are motivated by love (those who choose), most are motivated by fear (those who choose by not choosing)," she writes. On that vacation, I knew it was time to choose, and this time I did.

Every night, there was a gathering of the children beside a bonfire under the moon. When we got tired, we retreated to our cabin and held on to each other through the night and stayed in bed till the morning sun was high in the sky. The night before we left, we waded out onto the sandbars under the moonlight and discovered that we were making sparkling footsteps in the sand. We splashed water up onto the sand and swirled our hands, leaving behind traces of light on the bar.

I returned to the old house, where I met my children after they had returned from a vacation in Maine with my parents. I told them about the lights in the water in Bathurst, and one night after the sun set, we walked down to the beach with flashlights. When we turned off our flashlights, we watched the waves breaking on the beach and discovered that the foam was glowing in the dark. We splashed out into water that appeared to be sprinkled with tiny stars wherever we touched it. Where the water lay flat, it was dark. Where it was being agitated, it sparkled with light. As we moved through the water, our legs sent rings of glowing ripples shimmering along the surface. We threw handfuls of sand and seaweed out into the bay and watched light explode on the water. We turned our flashlights back on and shone them into the water. We knelt down, cupped our hands, picked up handfuls of water, and let it run through our fingers. We saw nothing but water. The light is in the sand, we told ourselves. Then we thought, No, it's in the foam. In the end, all we knew for certain was that light appeared when we stirred up the sea. Aaron said, "If you don't believe in magic, you won't believe in this."

The dome of the star-filled sky closed over the cove where we stood. We drenched ourselves in luminescent spray and spoke of how we were seeing light from stars that had long ago been extinguished, and how this, too, was magic. When we grew tired, we walked slowly back to the house, soaked to the skin. I later found out that the sparkling light we saw is called bioluminescence and is created by a species of microscopic organisms that appear in our waters mainly in July and August and for some reason emit light when they are disturbed. Fishermen who work at night often speak of the water "firing" when they see a school of fish moving or they drop their anchors and see lights flashing all the way to the bottom.

Samuel Coleridge wrote of the experience of witnessing bioluminescence in his "Rime of the Ancient Mariner."

Beyond the shadow of the ship
I watched the water-snakes:
They moved in tracks of shining white,
And when they reared, the elfish light
Fell off in hoary flakes.

Within the shadow of the ship
I watched their rich attire:
Blue, glossy green, and velvet black,
They coiled and swam; and every track
Was a flash of golden fire.

In the epigraph published with his poem, Coleridge quotes an observation from seventeenth-century English theologian Thomas Burnet that there are more invisible than visible beings in the universe and that at times we should allow our minds to contemplate their mysteries. "About such matters the human mind has always circled without attaining knowledge," Burnet writes. "Yet I do not doubt that sometimes it is well for the soul to contemplate as in a picture the image of a larger and better world, lest the mind, habituated by the small concerns of daily life, limit itself too much and sink entirely into trivial thinking."

Spending those ten days with Deb on the shore, watching those children dancing under the moon and discovering the magic lights in the water, took us out of trivial thinking. It was a cleansing, a giant lesson in perspective. I was broke, but not broken, and I was as happy as I had ever been in my life. There is never a point in our lives where we can declare that we have suffered all we will suffer, but there are times when we are offered a chance to refill ourselves with hope.

21

Years later, Walter insists the dark year was in many ways not so dark, that there was more clarity for him in the months we spent together in the old house than in all the years of his marriage and travelling the world that preceded them. At some point, he woke up during the dark year and started really feeling and seeing the world, even if what he was seeing was at times painful. I know that I was so wrapped up in my own troubles that I didn't notice how hard that year was for my brother, especially those long, lonely days he spent trying to turn the old house into a home.

I experienced a similar awakening. I remember days during the dark year as clearly as if they happened yesterday, while whole years of my life before the dark year have disappeared from my memory. My sister Susan also suffers from an almost complete memory loss of the years of her first marriage. I don't know how to account for my memory gap, whether to attribute it to nothing more than my failing memory or to the fact that I may not have been present enough in the small moments of each day to create a mental record of these years. I'm plagued by this amnesia, and because many of my lost years were during my children's early years, I know I have lost something I wish I could retrieve.

I had staggered and stumbled into the dark year and come out the other end walking steadily on my own two feet. Novelist Alistair

MacLeod, in *No Great Mischief*, his great novel of family ties, tells us that "all of us are better when we're loved." My brother, who as a boy had looked to me to lead us on our adventures on this shore, had as a man picked me up and carried me on his strong back until I was able to walk on my own and begin to rebuild my life. He had picked me up with his friendship and love, and I think at times I was able to offer him the same in return.

One morning in late August, I packed everything I could fit into the Toyota and left the old house and the dark year behind. I remember, as I drove down the driveway away from the house, seeing Walter standing alone on the porch, and a wave of sadness washed over me. I stepped on the brake and paused for a long moment, and then lifted my foot and swung the wheel away from the sea.

The Things Which Are

1

In the weeks after I left the old house, my former wife and I sold our farm in the St. John River valley. One morning early in the fall, the movers backed their trailer up the lane over a carpet of fallen leaves to carry away the boxes and furniture I had ended up with after the division of our belongings. The next day, I visited the farm one last time and spent the evening sweeping and mopping floors, wiping shelves and windowsills, and filling garbage bags with old newspapers, broken toys, mismatched shoes, and the general debris that remained in the corners of rooms and the backs of closets. Walter came with his truck to help me haul away the garbage. It was after midnight by the time I finished my cleaning. I took one more walk through the empty rooms, turning off lights and closing windows, preparing to leave the family home we had once believed would be our final destination.

I picked up my broom, mop, and bucket, stepped out on the porch, and locked the door behind me. I had cried over a lot of things during the past year and a half, but I wasn't about to cry over the farm. The dark year had taught me that the farmhouse, out-buildings, and gardens, meadows, and forest were only a stage set for a young couple's dreams. A physical place cannot transform a family into a happy family. A family home is found in the realm of the intangibles, in friendships and in love. I was ready for a new start.

Walter was leaning against his truck in the yard. I gave him a bear hug, and he drove away, heading south back to the old house. I drove down the lane for the last time and turned north through the river valley to the city of Fredericton, where my former wife had taken a new job and the children had enrolled in new schools. I would spend the weekend with Deb and meet the movers at my new home on Monday morning.

Two weeks earlier, I had bought a six-year-old bungalow on the outskirts of the city. I had worked in Fredericton some years ago as a newspaper reporter, and my boss, a gentle man named Glen Allen, used to tell me with a smile, "It's a sleepy, sleepy town," before sending me home early on Friday afternoons, much to the dismay of the editors who were trying to fill a Saturday edition with stories. Glen was right. The capital city of the province, with its two universities and a population of bureaucrats, academics, and students, is a sleepy town compared to the rugged, rough-and-tumble seaport city an hour to the south where I grew up.

Fredericton's neighbourhoods of painted clapboard homes and competitive gardens line the flood plains and hillsides of the green river valley. In the days when I worked with Glen in our little newspaper office downtown, I had everything I needed within walking distance. I walked downriver to the provincial legislature, the theatre, and the art gallery and upriver to the justice building, the city hall, and an array of downtown shops. Between our office and the river, the city had converted an abandoned railway bed into a system of walking and biking trails that crossed the river on what had been a train bridge and continued north through the St. John River valley and southeast into the valley of the Nashwaak River, which drains into the main river just below Fredericton's downtown.

When I bought the bungalow on the city's outskirts, I was trying to simplify my life. For the first time, I had bought a house because it was what I needed right then, on the very day I bought it. My cash flow was being gobbled up by debt and child support payments. I could manage to finance a house — but not a lifetime project. I considered living downtown, but I wasn't ready to give up on the idea of country living and I figured I could get more house for my money outside the city. I settled on a place about twenty minutes north of the downtown on a ridge that overlooks an inlet of the main river.

The house was a side-split bungalow with grey vinyl siding. There were three bedrooms with a large bathroom downstairs for the kids, a living room, and TV room on opposite sides of the kitchen, and three bedrooms and another full bathroom upstairs, where I would set up my bedroom and writing room. The bungalow had been built back off the road in the centre of a two-acre lot and was surrounded by mature cedars, pines and spruce, maples, ash, and white birch. I had neighbours on all sides but could catch only glimpses of their houses through the trees in winter when the leaves had fallen. In summer, we were completely enclosed by our little forest. Deb, who lived in the city, five minutes from coffee shops and newsstands and a social life, told me I had arranged for everything but the moat.

On Monday morning, while I was waiting for the moving truck to arrive, I walked around the yard and then out to the edge of the lot, where the leaves on the hardwood trees had turned red and orange and the trunks and branches were creaking in the wind. For the first time in a long time, I felt like I was bringing some order to my life. When the movers finished unloading, I left the boxes unopened in piles and drove to a furniture store in the city where I bought three single beds for the kids and a fold-out futon couch for the TV room. I stopped to pick up a load of groceries and returned to start assembling the bones of a new family home.

I had no guide for how to conduct myself as a parent during

these days. I purchased an aftermath-of-divorce self-help library, and I kept in the back of my mind the stories Deb had told me of how her father conducted himself in the years after her parents divorced. Deb and I grew up on the bookends of the no-fault divorce revolution. I was born in 1963, and in my neighbourhood, few of my friends had parents who were divorced. Deb was born in 1970, and by the time she was a teenager, no-fault divorce laws had been passed in Canada and the United States and most of her friends had been touched by family divisions in some way. She was sixteen when her parents separated, and she stayed at home with her mother while her older brother moved into a new house across town with her father.

Deb told me that after her parents separated her father would call her every morning, often waking her up early on school days. On weekends, he would pick her up for breakfast or a beach walk, and he would invite her and her friends over for Sunday dinners. In the winter, he would organize ski vacations and allow her to invite a friend. She told me how important it was to her that he reached out to her during her teenage years, even if she resisted his attention most of the time. Through his daughter's stories, Timothy Nobes became my role model as I worked at maintaining connections to my children. I called them every day and tried to be there for them whether they said they needed me or not. I did all the driving from my house to their mom's house. Some days, I know I drove them all crazy.

A couple of months after I moved into the bungalow, I left my newspaper job to write a biography of a former premier of New Brunswick. My plan was to finish writing the book in about a year, during which time we would live off the advance I had received from my publisher until I could find another job. I knew that if worst came to worst, I could keep us afloat as a freelance writer. On research and interview days, I was out running the roads, but on writing days, I worked alone in the silence of the bungalow, my computer and notes spread out on an old pine table. In the afternoons when I was too sleepy to write well, I walked the dogs through the quiet streets of our rural neighbourhood to the river for a swim.

After I moved to Fredericton, Deb and I starting spending more time together. She would drive out to my new house, or I would drive into the city to meet her. We enjoyed this time, but each step forward was careful and tentative, like we were walking across a fragile surface that might crack under our weight at any moment.

The children arrived for the three days a week they were to spend with me and filled the house with life. The big living room with a cathedral ceiling had so little furniture they converted it into an indoor badminton court, while the basement became a floor hockey and roller skating venue. They spread their school books on the floor of the TV room, started running endless loads of laundry, and monopolized the phone line for hours.

When the nights grew colder and the snow fell, I cleared a space beside the house and made an outdoor rink, hanging floodlights in the trees so we could play hockey after dark. On nights when it was cold enough to make ice, I boiled a kettle of water to thaw the outside tap, hooked up the hose, and watered the little rink. The secret to making smooth and solid ice is to take it slow, spreading a thin layer of water each time, allowing the previous layer to freeze solid before applying the next. A good backyard rink is never created in one night of flooding. I learned by trial and error that if I rushed it and poured on too much water at once, the ice would be rough, with air pockets that would chip and break, and it would take several more nights to repair the damage I created in my one night of haste. Flooding a backyard rink is an exercise in patience, in slowing down and taking it one cold night at a time until the layers of water create a solid and smooth platform for a game. Ice-making is all about good maintenance.

We all skated on the rink, but Aaron was out there skating and shooting the puck from the moment he came home from school until it was time for bed, with just a short break for dinner. Deb took a photograph of ten-year-old Aaron in full flight on our little rink and later gave it to me in a frame. In the photograph, he is wearing a black toque, hooded sweatshirt, and black hockey gloves. He is holding his stick in his left hand, the blade sliding across the ice, his whole body turned toward the puck he is chasing. He is so beautiful in that moment, on the ice of our new family home that we were building one careful layer at a time.

2

Late in the winter, my former wife — searching for a new start — moved to the United States to look for a new job, and the kids moved into the house with me full-time. I can't describe the hurt, loss, and anxiety my children were experiencing during this time in their lives because to suggest in any way that I understand what they were going through would be to trivialize their experience. I do know they were innocent bystanders — first in the divorce, and now the separation of their parents by a great physical divide. I had made the decisions I had made, and my former wife had made another decision that she thought she had to make. The children were dealing with the hard consequences of these decisions. In the beginning, I worked through all of the usual rationalizations to try to come to terms with what had happened to our family in the last year and a half.

I told myself that I had to make myself happy in order to be a good father to my children, that we would get through all of this big hurt and we would be stronger for it in the end. I picked up the well-used line of the no-fault divorce era, that staying married for the sake of the kids would have subjected them to life in an unhappy household, which would have been worse than what they went through during the divorce. It took me a long time to admit that while there is an element of truth in all these rationalizations, they aren't entirely honest. Divorce is always agonizing for children. I had made a decision that hurt the people I care for most in the world. I believed I had no choice if I was to continue living with myself.

Years later, when I asked students in writing workshops to describe a turning point in their lives, inevitably several people would describe their parents' divorce as the most painful period. I always found their stories difficult to read, because they served as reminders of what a terrible time this was for my children and how they, too, would see their parents' divorce as the event that shaped their destiny, as much as the happy memories of their childhood.

In the end, I had to acknowledge that the pain I brought to the lives of my former wife and my children was not collateral damage. It was a direct hit. When I faced up to this fundamental truth, I was left wrestling with the question of how I could reconcile my desire for a different kind of love and happiness in my own life with the suffering I had caused in my family. How could this be considered anything but a reckless, selfish, and callous way to live? Would I not have been a better man if I had put the needs of others before my pursuit of love and second chances? How could my pursuit of happiness be considered something good when the most obvious manifestation of it in the lives of the people I loved was hardship and loss?

When we strip away the modern self-help rationalizations, we come to the heart of a question that dominated the earliest literature in the western tradition. George Dimock constructs his reading of *The Odyssey* around this very question and his translation of the name of Odysseus, which he associates with the verb *odyssasthai*, which means to will pain to another. Odysseus is "the man of pain," whose decision to fight the war at Troy for ten years and then spend another ten years making his way home caused enormous suffering for his wife, Penelope, and their son, Telemachus;

for his mother, who died during his absence; and for his father, who mourned the loss of his son every day he was gone and became a hermit because of it. The journey of Odysseus resulted in the deaths of all his crew members, which caused their families to suffer. When he arrived home at long last, he slaughtered the suitors of Penelope who had occupied his house and the maids who slept with the suitors, and these families in turn mourned the deaths of their daughters and sons.

How could the man who caused so much pain be a hero worthy of our admiration? The simple answer, according to Dimock, is because this pain is what living is about. We live, inevitably cause pain to others, and in turn bring pain upon ourselves. Yet how can the pursuit of happiness be so closely associated with the pain of living?

"Men have always wondered why the world is not a more comfortable place," Dimock writes. "The author of the account in Genesis realizes that to live in paradise would mean having to do without the knowledge of good and evil, but seems to consider such ignorance an advantage. Homer disagrees. He can see no real happiness in a world free of danger and hardship and work and a final end in death. To be hidden in the midst of the sea with Kalypso might well mean to be free of these things. Homer made it mean that. But could a man really enjoy such freedom? Homer's narrative makes us feel more strongly than any argument that one could not enjoy this paradise, this freedom from mortality, without losing what is most precious about being human. To be human is to accept 'evil,' all those things one calls bad, as one's lot, and that is what Odysseus is doing as he leaves Kalypso to cross the dangerous sea."

Odysseus has willed pain to the people he loves most in the world, in particular Telemachus when he left him at home. Odysseus is a leader and a warrior, he is who he is, and Homer makes no apologies for his decision to join the Greek army at Troy.

However, the poet shows us just how painful this decision was when Odysseus finally lands on the shores of Ithaca and encounters his son, who was just an infant when he left. When they recognize each other, they fall into an embrace and weep.

> *Odysseus sat down again, and Telemachus threw his arms*
> *around his great father, sobbing uncontrollably*
> *as the deep desire for tears welled up in both.*
> *They cried out, shrilling cries, pulsing sharper*
> *than birds of prey — eagles, vultures with hooked claws —*
> *When farmers plunder their nest of young too young to fly.*

The love of father and child, and the pain brought on by their separation, is immediate, instinctive, like that of wild birds in the field. I read those words when I was preparing to teach a section on *The Odyssey* in the Great Books program at St. Thomas University, a small liberal arts university in Fredericton, and the day I read it I emailed the passage to my father and told him how afraid I was that I might lose my children if they ended up living with their mom somewhere far away from me. I was afraid that my own mid-life odyssey as a man of pain might bring down upon me the great unspoken fear that all parents hold deep in their hearts: that their children will be lost to them before they are old enough to fly.

Staying together for the sake of the children might make sense for some people and indeed might be the most reasonable solution for many troubled marriages. In my case, I would have either had to be dishonest about my feelings or had to pursue happiness outside the marriage and live some kind of parallel life. I would never presume to question someone who made such a choice, but the simple fact is I couldn't do it. This doesn't make me a better man. It just makes me who I am. I made my choice, and I had to accept my lot.

I tried to push my fears about the future to the back of my mind and to accept that I could control only the events within my reach. The best thing, the only thing, I could do for us was to make our new home as peaceful and safe and loving as it could be. I tried to cook good meals and keep the house clean and be present for my children when they needed me. I reminded myself every day that all I could control was how I conducted myself, which was with as much patience and calm as I could bring to a house filled with two teenage girls and a preteen boy. I had my hands full. All of my energy went into keeping the household running smoothly. Many days I settled for just keeping it running.

The girls could take the bus to their schools in the city, but Aaron had to be driven back and forth because there was no bus to take him to his, and I didn't want him to have to change schools. I was up early every morning packing three lunches, sometimes four if the kids had a friend staying overnight as they often did, knocking on bedroom doors and mediating arguments over length of bathroom use. The girls generally came with us in the car, and we always tried to have a good laugh during the morning drives. For months the laughs revolved around a foolish radio contest called "the rock sandwich," which involved guessing which three song clips made up the sandwich. The station played oldies, so I always guessed the bread and the filling correctly, and my kids made fun of me for being old enough to recognize these songs — which I countered by telling them I might quit writing and we could live off the proceeds of the contest. We were getting a lot of mileage out of a little cheesy morning humour, and in those days we needed all the fuel we could get.

I made time to write between those morning drives to school and the afternoon pickups, and I wrote again late in the evening after I'd finished washing the supper dishes, helping with homework, and running loads of laundry, when Aaron and the girls had retreated to their rooms for reading or sleep. In the late evening silence, I brewed fresh coffee and waited for yet another second wind and for my mind to fall into the story I was trying to tell, rather than wandering through the multitude of responsibilities that dominated my daily routine.

<h1 style="text-align:center">3</h1>

One weekend when my book-writing deadlines were closing in on me, I arranged for my parents to stay with the kids for the weekend while I rented a lake cottage as a work retreat. Deb agreed to keep me company. I loaded my boxes of research material into the Toyota, picked her up at her apartment, and drove to the lake. Without so much as a walk down to the shore, I unloaded the boxes, set up my laptop on the dining-room table, and went to work. I didn't want to waste a minute of this big open space of concentrated time that I hoped would allow me to finish a particularly difficult chapter. Sometime the next day, Deb had finished reading her first novel and was starting on her second. She was lying on the couch under a blanket when I stood up and stretched my arms to the ceiling to work the stiffness out of my back. I started toward the kitchen to make more coffee and called over my shoulder, "Do you need anything?"

"Yes," she replied. "I need a friend." I laughed, and then when I turned and started for the coffee pot again, I realized she wasn't laughing with me. I shut down the computer, pulled her up off the couch, and we drove into Saint John. We went out to dinner and shopped at an antiques sale, and on the drive back to the cabin we talked about the direction — or lack of direction — of our lives together and I promised I would try to be a better boyfriend. I knew I hadn't been much of a friend of any kind in recent months. If I wasn't writing, I was cooking, or cleaning the house, or coordinating some complicated drop-off-and-pickup schedule for my children's hockey and social events. I was carrying a pager on my belt so the kids could reach me, and the little device seemed to be vibrating day and night.

About the time I finished the final chapters of the book, I started teaching journalism courses at St. Thomas University, and then I started writing stories for the *Ottawa Citizen*. Once again I was consumed with so many little tasks that just scheduling my day was a challenge. Some months later, when the university offered me a full-time job to build a new journalism program, I decided this might be a chance to focus on one job and to really begin the process of remaking my life. I was ready for a makeover. I had been looking after many things, and had embraced the full-time dad routine, but between my work and my homemaking, I wasn't looking after myself and certainly not caring for my relationship with Deb. She was discouraged about our prospects. Too often our only conversations were telephone calls late in the evening when we were both too tired to make much sense other than to remind each other that love is a verb.

The St. Thomas University campus is located near the top of the highest hill in the city. When I reported for work in late summer and stood in the main courtyard admiring the commanding view of the downtown streets, the steeple of the Anglican cathedral, the greens of summer, and the splashes of blue in the river valley, I thought that perhaps I had come to a place where I could truly bring some order to my life after a series of false starts. I felt the warm August sun on my face and closed my eyes for a minute and rested. I was so tired.

4

Soon after I arrived on campus, I met an old friend, Barry Craig, who had studied classics with me at Dalhousie. Barry was a few years ahead of me in his studies, but we often shared coffee in the musty lounge in the Dalhousie classics house, an old Halifax residence converted into classrooms and offices, where we participated in wide-ranging conversations about Greek philosophy, St. Augustine, and Dante. We believed that somewhere in these volumes and conversations we would come to understand the nature of a virtuous life.

The classics department was a forgotten little world on a campus where most administrative attention and financial resources were directed toward the prestigious schools of law and medicine. Most of the graduate courses I took had fewer than half a dozen students. We met in tiny, smoke-filled classrooms on the main level of the house or sometimes in the upstairs office of the professor who taught the class.

The department shared its faculty with King's College, a High Church Anglican liberal arts institution associated with the main university, where Deb had studied journalism. Our department was staffed by socialist survivors of the back-to-the land movement, eccentric European intellectuals, and buttoned-down Anglican conservatives. Barry was more closely associated with the buttoned-down crowd. He looked the part with his short-back-and-sides haircut, his jacket and tie, although he never took himself too seriously and spent hours in the lounge holding court as he made fun of the strange intellectual culture and often incomprehensible language of the dialogue in our little department.

After he completed his studies, Barry became an Anglican priest, and I heard he had been running a parish in the Miramichi River town of Blackville in central New Brunswick. When I met him in the courtyard, he told me in a rush of words that he was married and had three young children. He was preaching at an Anglican parish in Fredericton and teaching philosophy full-time at St. Thomas. In fact, he was teaching an overload of courses and completing his doctorate in philosophy. When I asked him how he was handling all this, and whether he was happy in this impossibly busy situation, he told me that he was "excellent," an expression of his that I remembered from our graduate days. Then he flashed me a big smile and hurried off to attend some meeting or other. As he disappeared around a corner lugging his heavy briefcase, I thought that he was running awfully hard, and in him I recognized myself from not so long ago.

I saw Barry from time to time on campus, but we were always too busy to do more than stop for five-minute conversations. Some months later, I was sitting on a bench in the courtyard having a coffee with a friend and we watched Barry hurrying by in the distance with an armload of books. My friend told me that there was gossip swirling around campus that his personal life was in chaos. I listened, but all I said in response was that I was sorry, and I left it at that. I'm often the last to hear these kinds of stories because I never have anything to give back; it's not much fun for a gossip to give and not receive.

As a journalist, I learned long ago that while there is a value in listening to gossip, because occasionally the seeds of stories can be found in the chatter, there is never any value in dispensing it. I also learned that there are many sides to a story, and having been the subject of a variety of inaccurate scandal stories after my marriage ended, I tend not to believe much of what I hear. As a former editor liked to tell me when I was a young reporter, many a good story has been ruined by over-verification. I watched Barry disappear at the top of the courtyard with his armload of books and decided that he would come to me if he wanted to talk.

5

One weekend in September, I decided to take Deb fly fishing for Atlantic salmon on the Miramichi River to celebrate her birthday. When I asked her if she wanted to go fly fishing, she reluctantly agreed to give it a try. Her only fishing experience had been a deep-sea fishing weekend with her former boyfriend and some of his pals. I had heard stories about this trip, about their departure in a big red and white Cadillac loaded with coolers of beer, and how later that day she was the only one sober enough to drive, though she wasn't allowed to back up the Cadillac because the owner didn't trust a female driver. She told me how she cooked dinner for everyone in the cabin and washed all the dishes, and how she had been generally annoyed and angry about the entire experience. She went on the trip only because her boyfriend, also a journalist, had just published an exposé about an RCMP informant who allegedly got away with murder, among other heinous things, and who was in trouble with both the police and a couple of biker gangs. Days before the story was published, this informant had wandered intentionally past the house Deb shared with her boyfriend, so she refused to stay in the house alone while the boys went fishing.

I have been on these kinds of trips before and they aren't about fishing. All I really remember about them is the hangovers. While my fishing partners slept theirs off, I would be out casting my line with a searing headache and bad stomach, doing what my father taught me to do whenever I was near fish, namely to get my line in the water and try to catch one. I had stopped going on the boys' trips a long time ago.

I had something different in mind on the cool September morning we drove northeast from the city into the sprawling Miramichi River drainage, which dominates the geography of central New Brunswick. Our destination was a little town called Boiestown — a community built alongside the river where you can buy a fishing rod and waders along with your bread and milk at the general store — and a stretch of river fished by my friend Renate Bullock, who is a fishing guide. Renate lives in a log house on a high bank above one of the best pools on the Miramichi River system. I had met Renate several years earlier when I interviewed her for a series of stories I was writing about salmon river conservation. The morning I arrived at her house, we ended up spending a day on the water. I listened to her river stories and watched one of the most accomplished fly casters I had ever seen work a stretch of water she knew intimately.

When I was in the worst of the turmoil of my divorce, I travelled to the river, sat on the bank with Renate, and told her the whole story. Without a hint of judgment, she said she understood that I had to do what I needed to do to keep on living and that we all need true friendship and love in our lives.

I took Deb to Boiestown because I wanted her to meet my friend, and I wanted Renate to be at Deb's side when she took her first steps out into the river. If there was any chance for her to hook a fish that day, her odds would increase a hundred-fold with my best guide directing the day's events.

Renate outfitted Deb in a set of waders and a fly rod and took her out on the water, stood beside her in the current, and showed her the ten o'clock to two o'clock, three-beat motion of fly casting. With the current swirling around her boots and her line moving across the water, Deb began to understand why I long for such days on the river, in the swirls and eddies, waiting for a fish to rise.

About ten o'clock, we all stopped casting for a coffee break. We sat on the bank and watched the pool and the occasional jumping fish while Renate went up to her kitchen and brought back a carafe of freshly brewed coffee and a tin of blueberry crumb cake she had baked the night before. We all fell into conversation and had a good rest until we felt like wading back out to begin casting again. Late in the morning, Deb hooked a salmon that ran, stripped line off her reel, and jumped in the sunlight in a flash of silver and spray. With Renate coaching her, Deb brought the fish to the net and then released it back into the river. For the rest of the day she couldn't wipe the huge grin off her face. After that trip, we visited a fly fishing shop and Deb bought herself a pair of waders and a rod. That birthday trip to the Miramichi River became the first of many river trips. My river friends became Deb's friends, and slowly, without any real agenda, we began to move into common spaces where we could enjoy each other's presence and share in and support each other's passions. It had given us hope that in the midst of all of the competing interests in our lives, perhaps we could carve out some space for each other.

6

The following spring, Deb moved into our bungalow on the outskirts of the city. I continued to be consumed most of the time by running the household, so if Deb and I were going to make a life together, we needed to be living in the same space. I was anxious about taking this step because change is never easy. The kids had met Deb and had spent time with her both at our house and at her apartment in the city and they enjoyed her company and friendship. However, we knew creating a new family arrangement was a different matter altogether. My kids and I had a functioning household, and upsetting it carried a certain amount of risk. Moreover, Deb was used to living alone, and she would be living in a household where she was not in control of her environment. But I was ready, because I had kept my personal promise to learn to stand alone before I began a life with another. I had proven to myself that I could be a full-time writer and teacher and dad, that I could be self-sufficient. I was moving into this new phase of my life with Deb not because I needed her to help me make it through my days, but because I wanted her close to me. She made me happy, and I hoped I could make her happy too.

Before the moving van arrived with her belongings, I had all the carpets shampooed and I cleared out the upstairs bedroom that had been my writing room so she could create her own space, with a desk, a couch, and her piano. I figured that while she adjusted to living in a house filled with teenagers, she would need a place to read, play her piano, and just take a break from the action. I moved my piles of papers and books into the smaller room across the hall and cleared out two closets for her clothes and shoes. Gabby and a friend spent the morning making space in the kitchen cupboards for Deb's dishes.

The first months of creating a new family structure are a test for everyone involved. We knew the transition would be difficult, and it was. Among other things, we now had three dogs. The kids and I had an excitable Jack Russell terrier named Jake and a beagle-like mutt named Joey. Deb brought with her another mutt, a stubborn old lady dog named Isabella Rossellini, whom we all called Riz. We realized this pack was at least two dogs too many when they went tearing through the house that first day, the boys marking their territory inside and out, competing for top-dog spot. Riz was unhappy and started crawling under Gabby's bed at night and trying to scratch her way out of the house through the carpet. She was driving Gabby crazy, keeping her awake at night and reminding all of us of the general disruption.

For months Riz would stand by the front door and wait for her master to take her back to their apartment in town, where everything was nice and quiet and just as they liked it. She was openly hostile to me. Old dogs don't grin and bear it or learn to make the best of it. Perhaps Riz was the only truly honest one among us.

In the early days of our new family arrangement, I tried to be the great mediator who would help everyone sing in harmony when the discord grew too loud. Finally, after failing as choir director time and again, I stepped aside to let everyone find their own places. I realized that Deb, Aaron, and the girls would develop their own relationships, and I had absolutely no control over that.

Through the first months of a difficult transition, we never even considered giving up. Deb is a strong and determined person who doesn't allow a grievance to last more than a couple days. That summer, Deb and I started digging flowerbeds in front of the house. We planted some bright annuals to get us started, but Deb's main interest was in planning a perennial garden so we would have new flowers the following spring — we would allow ourselves to plan that far ahead. I made a trellis out of old cedar slab wood, and we planted a purple clematis and two grapevines that grew up either side. Out on the edges of the yard beneath the big trees, Deb designed a shade garden where we hung a new hammock between a cedar and a giant spruce. And so we moved forward, through one season into the next.

7

My father had helped me to understand that life is by nature difficult. When I was a teenager, my father gave me a copy of psychiatrist Scott Peck's bestselling *The Road Less Traveled: A New Psychology of Love, Traditional Values and Spiritual Growth* and told me that its opening lines would change my life if I took them to heart. "Life is difficult," Peck writes. "This is a great truth, one of the greatest truths. It is a great truth because once we truly see this truth, we transcend it. Once we truly know that life is difficult — once we truly understand and accept it — then life is no longer difficult. Because once it is accepted, the fact that life is difficult no longer matters." Of course I ignored these words as a teenager and figured it was my father who was trying to make my life difficult. When the dark year was upon me, I dug through my piles of books until I found Peck and read it cover to cover, in particular the chapter on love, where he writes: "I define love thus: The will to extend one's self for the purpose of nurturing one's own or another's spiritual growth." He defines love not as dependence on another person, but as a choice of free individuals to love each other because it is good for the person who is doing the loving and for the person receiving the love.

It was some time later that I noticed a footnote in his chapter on love, in which Peck writes that he had reached the conclusion that the only kind of marriage that was not ultimately destructive for a couple is an open marriage that promotes the individualism and separateness of the partners, as opposed to a closed marriage that requires partners to approach every aspect of life as a couple. He acknowledged that he was using the language of the controversial book *Open Marriage* by George and Nena O'Neill, published in 1972, just as the storm clouds began to engulf the institution of marriage.

"Open marriage means an honest and open relationship between two people, based on the equal freedom and identity of both partners. It involves a verbal, intellectual and emotional commitment to the right of each to grow as an individual within a marriage," the O'Neills write. "In a closed relationship, the couple does not exist in a one-plus-one relationship. Their ideal is to become fused into a single entity — a couple. Separate experiences, beyond those forced upon them by the fact that the husband goes to an office or a factory while the wife remains home to clean and shop, are not allowed except for the occasional, generally resented outings with 'the Boys' (for the husband) and 'the Girls' (for the wife)." My first marriage had been a kind of closed relationship, and I knew that's not what I wanted with Deb, and it wasn't what she wanted with me.

We were together but separate, and we fiercely protected our independence. Our finances were kept separate. We collected receipts for household expenses in a cookie tin and settled up at the end of each month. We had our own cars and our own insurance companies. I kept the house in my name and Deb helped with a percentage of the mortgage payments.

At the same time that we were protecting our separate spaces, we were striving to create the kind of intimacy that German psychologist Erik Erikson regarded as the highest end of our development as young adults. Dr. Covert told me one day how

Erikson developed a theory of our psychosocial development, as an alternative to Sigmund Freud's theory of psychosexual development. According to Erikson, we have a series of developmental milestones we need to reach at various stages in our lives. In infancy, we develop trust; in adolescence, identity. As young adults, our objective should be to allow ourselves to experience intimacy. In middle adulthood, our objective should be what Erikson calls generativity, which he defines as working to make the world a better place for future generations. As adults, if we are not able to have intimacy or generativity in our lives, we end up living a life of isolation and stagnation. Intimacy is the condition that allows us to connect, feel attached, secure, and trust the person we are closest to. We trust this person with all of ourself.

Philosopher Bertrand Russell wrote eloquently about this kind of intimacy in his groundbreaking *Marriage and Morals*, published in 1929, which argues for the freeing of women from the constraints imposed on them by marriage and Victorian morality. He also advocates sex before marriage and even trial marriages before the contract is signed, all daring and controversial ideas in their day. "The essence of a good marriage is respect for each other's personality combined with that deep intimacy, physical, mental, and spiritual, which makes a serious love between a man and a woman the most fructifying of all human experiences," Russell writes. "Such love, like everything that is great and precious, demands its own morality, and frequently entails of a sacrifice of the less to the greater; but such sacrifice must be voluntary, for, where it is not, it will destroy the very basis of the love for the sake of which it is made."

In *Open Marriage*, the O'Neills gently suggest that some couples may be able to negotiate an open sexual relationship as a condition of an open marriage. However, the book does not recommend it, just states matter-of-factly that these kinds of relationships are possible. Scott Peck picks up the open sexual marriage theme and suggests that a person who has a great deal of self-discipline could pursue sexual relationships outside the marriage and still have a strong and nurturing partnership with his or her spouse. This observation puzzled me for a long time. I wondered how this man, who describes with such clarity the possibilities of a true love relationship, could advocate an arrangement that seemed to me to be ultimately destructive of any kind of loving relationship, at least for those of us who consider sex to be an essential part of an intimate relationship.

During one of my counselling sessions with Dr. Covert, she told me that when married men come to her and say they want to have an affair, she tells them to go ahead and have the affair if that's what they want to do. But then she asks them if they are going to feel guilty and have to go home and confess to their wives. If they feel the need to confess, she tells them they probably shouldn't have the affair.

Honesty is probably a good thing, but the primary requirement when we grow up is that we have relationships with equals, relationships in which there is the possibility of real intimacy. If we are intimate with one person, if we are truly attached, there is no room for someone else, she told me. That doesn't mean we can't be attracted to another person, but we wouldn't pursue such a relationship, or two-time them both, because then an intimate relationship isn't possible with either person.

This is where Scott Peck's argument for an open sexual marriage, even among the most disciplined of men and women, begins and ends. In the kind of relationship Peck imagines, a person might find friendship and intimacy at one time or another, but the intimacy would be fleeting at best.

Dr. Covert helped me to understand that I had lost the ability to be intimate with another, if I had ever really had it. I had never fully given myself over to another person, trusting that person with myself. I was able to give myself over to my work without reservations, but even there I was a relentless perfectionist, expecting more of myself than I needed to give. She told me I had the opportunity to change the patterns of my life. "It's very important to learn from your mistakes or you will repeat them," Dr. Covert reminded me. "We're creatures of habit," she said. "It's a real challenge to say, No, I don't want to be like this, this is not a good way to be, and then to say, Let's try to change it."

I later discovered that Scott Peck had struggled to live the disciplined life he advocates in *The Road Less Traveled*. In fact, he had never travelled on this road at all as far as love and marriage were concerned. He worked too hard, admitted that he neglected his children, and had many sexual relationships with women outside of his marriage. He was divorced from his wife, Lily, in the final years of his life. As discouraging as this story appears to be, perhaps there is a lesson in Peck's life and work. Life is difficult. True love is hard to find and sustain. A good marriage requires more than a solid theoretical base. "In a number of ways, I don't understand who I am," Peck said in an interview late in his life with *Psychology Today* magazine. "I'm somebody who often, like so many people, preaches what he needs to learn." Bertrand Russell had his own trials in his search for intimacy. He was married four times. Saying it is easy. Living it is another matter altogether.

8

Late that summer, when the children were away visiting with their mother at her new home in the southern United States, Deb and I made plans to go on a canoeing and camping vacation. It had been a difficult spring and summer: struggling to make our new living arrangement work, winning some days and losing others, finding most of our time consumed by the hurry of day-to-day living. We needed to get away together, to find each other again. I figured that we would be able to come together without distraction in natural spaces.

Howell Raines, the former editor of the *New York Times*, wrote in his mid-life reflection on rivers and fly fishing that, like many southerners, he was "ruined for church by over exposure to preachers" in his youth. He found spiritual enlightenment on rivers, the places where he could hear the "sigh of the Eternal." I, too, was overexposed to preachers in my youth — mainly in my father's church.

However, father also exposed me to natural spaces, in particular rivers and streams on the countless fishing trips we made. In the end, I chose the rushing waters as my church, although I respect and admire my father's work in both places. Deb and I planned to canoe and fish a river I had run before with my father: the Patapédia, along the border of New Brunswick and Quebec.

I knew Deb and I needed this trip, and I wanted it to happen, but I had become so wrapped up in making everything work at home for so long that I had trouble leaving it. My anxiety level increased as the departure day grew closer, and I transferred my worries into fussing over our gear. We would be three days on the river and planned to continue camping after that, and I began to obsessively plan for the trip. For days I piled gear in the living room, made long lists, and then misplaced them and wrote new ones, and then packed and repacked the car. We finally pulled out of the driveway with a carload of gear, pulling my old canoe on a trailer, with Deb telling me to stop worrying and let the trip happen or she might have to put me out on the side of the road and go it alone. We drove north to the city of Campbellton, where we bought our final load of groceries and ice, then crossed the Restigouche River bridge and drove into the Quebec town of Matapédia, where we planned to register for our trip and make arrangements to hire someone to drive our car around to the place where we would pull out.

When we arrived, the registration office in Matapédia was closed for the afternoon; the sign on the door said it would reopen early in the evening. I knew we would be hard pressed to get to the river before dark. My best laid plans were crumbling all around me. I was nervously pacing in the parking lot when Deb suggested that I should take this opportunity to see how all the gear would fit into the canoe. I thought that was an excellent idea and spent an hour or so loading and unloading the canoe while Deb found some shade in a corner of the parking lot, where she spread out a camping mat, read her book, took a long nap, and awoke even more refreshed and relaxed.

We did make it to the river before dark. My worries slipped away into the still night air, replaced by the sound of the current running over gravel bars in the river. We pushed off in the morning, swept downstream by the water, which from that point dictated the pace of the trip. The first night we camped beside the best salmon pool on the river, a place called Swimming Hole. We unloaded our gear in a clearing on the bank where the rapids run into a deep salmon holding pool. After we pitched the tent and set up camp, we stripped and swam in the icy waters, then lit the camp stove, cooked dinner, drank a bottle of wine, and watched the salmon jumping and rolling in the pool. Then a couple of hours before the sun set, we pulled on our boots and went fishing. That evening, Deb hooked a large salmon that ran fifty metres downriver and jumped and splashed and stripped line off her reel until I netted it in the slack waters beside our campsite and then released it back into the strong currents of the river.

Deb and I spent the following two days fishing and floating in the canoe. When we grew tired of paddling, we stopped to rest on gravel beaches, where we brewed coffee and Deb read to me. I rested and listened to the sound of her voice mingling with the music of the water flowing past us.

On the afternoon of our third day, we beached the canoe about a mile upriver from our car, opened our last bottle of wine, and fried trout that we had caught earlier that afternoon. We had planned on spending one more night in a cabin at the pullout spot. When we arrived at the cabin just before dusk, we found the door locked and no one anywhere in the vicinity to ask for a key. We considered setting up our tent and camping, but the black flies were out in full force, so we loaded our gear in the back of the car, pulled the canoe onto the trailer, and drove down narrow logging roads in the dark toward civilization. Several hours later, we were crawling into a warm and dry bed in a room at a Holiday Inn and told ourselves that, in fact, this was exactly where we needed to be.

We took a couple of hours in the morning to shower, dry our gear in the parking lot, and repack the Toyota. Then we drove off across the top of the province toward Kouchibouguac National Park on the shore of Northumberland Strait with no plans other than to do some camping and explore the coastline. The park is small in the order of national parks, just two hundred or so square miles of salt marshes, mudflats, saltwater lagoons, and sand dunes that surround the lazy tidal waters of the Kouchibouguac River. This park is surely one of the great little-travelled places in North America, with the warmest sea water north of the Carolinas in the lagoons and mile after mile of white sand beaches.

We arrived at the park late in the afternoon. After we'd bought a wilderness camping permit, we filled our water jugs with fresh water. Then we launched the canoe into the river at a fishing wharf and paddled toward a remote campsite at the mouth of the river. Our alternate destination, if we were really feeling adventurous, was a large dune farther offshore that allowed wilderness camping. When we reached the campground on the point and looked out across an expanse of ocean at the dune a couple miles away, we decided in an instant that we would keep going. We paused long enough to drink a beer and eat a snack of canned herring and crackers and pushed off again.

We landed on the dune as the sun was setting and set up our tent at the edge of the beach. For the next two days, we camped alone on a seven-mile-long dune, with no visitors except an occasional boatload of picnickers and a group of seals that assembled just offshore and watched our every move. There were hundreds of seals in these waters, where they gathered on smaller dunes to mate in the summer. Our group of seals had broken away from a larger herd that we could hear moaning and bellowing farther away. The seals reminded us of curious dogs, their heads bobbing up and down out of the water, obsessively monitoring the movements of these two strangers and their bright blue tent. The seals were there in the early morning when I rose to light a fire and boil tea and watch the lobster boats motor out of the mouth of the river, and they were there when we left our fire in the evening and crawled into our sleeping bags in the tent. When the winds subsided, which wasn't often out on the edge of the Atlantic Ocean, we launched the canoe and paddled around the shore to observe a large colony of mating seals on smaller offshore dunes. The rest of the time we sunbathed and read each other books, and swam naked in the sea. We had found each other again on the river, and on the dune we discovered an intimacy we had never known, physical, emotional, and intellectual. We were there together, framed only by the sand and sea under a big blue New Brunswick sky.

When we'd had all we could take of the wind blowing sand in our food, we broke camp, loaded the canoe one last time, and paddled back to the mainland. We found a cabin just outside the park where we rested for two days, and when we drove home from our great adventure, we were filled up with each other, ready to face any trials that might come upon us.

9

That fall and winter, we began to address the question of where the children would live as their primary residence while they went to school. I did everything I could to keep my children in New Brunswick for as long as I could. Over time, I earned a shadow degree in family law and learned that fathers almost always face an uphill battle in these situations. All of this is an ugly business, and when lawyers who work in an adversarial system join forces with hired-gun social workers and psychologists, families can be drawn into a process that causes such great emotional and financial trauma that all participants lose in some fashion. Everyone has to make a living, but I have had a hard time forgiving some of the professionals who made good money from my family's misfortune. After these psychologists and social workers filed their reports, they washed their hands of our lives and never contacted us again, even though their interventions helped to decide the destiny of our family. As Cool Hand Luke reminds us, calling it your job don't make it right, boss.

By now, the girls were old enough to make their own decisions about where they would live, so in the end there was nothing for me to do but tell them that I would respect their decisions and continue to love them no matter what they chose to do. Gabby left to live with her mother in North Carolina the summer after Deb and I ran the river and camped on the dune. The morning she left, we sat together on the couch in the living room waiting for her ride to arrive, wrapped our arms around each other, and wept. We promised each other that morning that we would not to allow the distance to weaken our father-daughter bond, and we kept our promise. After she left, we talked on the phone almost every day. She would often call me as soon as she arrived home from school and we would review the events of our days as I cooked supper in the kitchen. In between phone calls, we wrote each other letters.

Hers would sometimes arrive perfumed and filled with confetti, little red, blue, and pink hearts spilling out of the corners of the envelope as I opened it.

The next summer, Danielle decided to spend her last year of high school in North Carolina and Aaron told me that that he needed to be with his mom and his sisters, and I agreed to let him go. He was twelve years old. It was either let him go or turn a legal skirmish into a war. I knew also that apart from his genuine desire to be with his mother and sisters, his decision was a courageous and selfless gesture. He knew his departure would end the conflict between his mother and me, and he was telling me without saying the words that he was confident enough in our love for each other that the move would not destroy what we had.

On a sunny morning in August, Danielle and Aaron loaded their bags into their mom's car and I stood in the yard and waved them away. When the car disappeared at the end of the drive, I sat down on the grass and had a good long cry, and then I went inside and washed the breakfast dishes, cleaned the three downstairs bedrooms, vacuumed the carpets, stripped my children's beds, washed and dried their sheets, and then remade the beds. Early in the evening, Deb took me to the movies. She was trying to keep me moving. I was sitting on a bench outside the theatre when my sister Susan arrived, having just driven into town to be there for me once again when the going got tough. She sat down on the bench and put her arms around me, hugging me for a long time. Then we got up and walked into the theatre.

There is a primal pain that emerges from a parent's separation from a child. Only those who have experienced it first-hand understand it fully. I have never found a way to properly express it in words. There are those who argue that fathers don't have the same nurturing instinct as mothers, that mothers instinctively understand the needs of children better than fathers do, that children need their mothers more than their fathers, and that some parents are primary caregivers and others secondary caregivers. I have been told all of these things by various psychologists and social workers, and all I can say in response is that they know not of what they speak.

I had been caught in a collision of two powerful loves. Tolstoy's *Anna Karenina* turns on this collision. The beautiful Anna has fallen in love with Vronsky and needs his love to feel alive, yet to be with him she must divorce her husband, Levin, and leave with him their son, Seryozha. She pleads with Levin to both grant her a divorce and allow her to live with their son. Levin refuses both requests. So Anna chooses to leave without a divorce to be with Vronsky, in a love she hoped would take up both *eros* and *philia*, desire and friendship, a decision that for her is ultimately tragic.

Like Anna, I had turned toward *eros* and *philia*, had chosen these loves as a necessary part of my life, and, like Anna, I had paid a price. I could sympathize with Anna's decision to throw herself in front of a moving train. When my children left, I became depressed. I couldn't sleep at night and was angry and sad during the day. I was unable to work productively. I started reading literature produced by the groups of men who had lost regular contact with their children after divorce, who have been campaigning for more rights for fathers in child custody cases. I considered joining this movement, of making connections with other sad and disillusioned men, and making it my life's work to correct these injustices. At the time, filled as I was with grief, I could think of no more noble a cause. When I told Deb of my plans, she told me in no uncertain terms that our lives could not be built around this kind of bitterness and sadness, however righteous the cause might be. I was free to go down that road, but I would be going it alone.

Because Deb recognized the depth of the hole I was in, she made me an appointment with a psychologist and told me I had to go if we were going to continue to make a life together. Slowly, with the help of a kind and thoughtful man whom I met on weeknights in a downtown office building, the depression began to lift. I began to accept what had happened and to allow myself to grieve what we had lost instead of railing against it in anger. Then I received an unexpected gift from my grandmother, who in the final act of her life allowed me to hope that while family love could stretch and strain, it could not be broken.

10

Three months after Danielle and Aaron joined Gabby in North Carolina, my mother's mother, Eda Carter Williams, whom we all called Biggie, suffered a stroke while out buying groceries with a friend. She was ninety-five years old. She died three days later. In the months before her death, she had told us that she was ready to die any time the call came. A family friend noted that she had died with her boots on, and that was no surprise to any of us.

Back in New Brunswick, it was Canadian Thanksgiving. Susan was in town for a visit. She joined Walter, Deb, and me at my parents' home to share a meal, to remember Biggie, and to start making arrangements to travel to Richmond, Virginia, for the funeral. Over the years, Biggie had organized family reunions by renting cottages at various summer resorts, even purchasing a beach house in Florida to attract her children and grandchildren for family gatherings. None of us knew that for years she had been planning to bring us together one last time. She had left instructions in her will ordering that her estate pay the travel costs for all of her children, grandchildren, and great-grandchildren to travel to Richmond to attend her funeral. We were her family, her blood as she liked to say, and we had long ago scattered to New York, California, Vermont, Michigan, New Brunswick, and Ontario. We boarded planes and trains for Richmond to bury Biggie and celebrate our last great family reunion. We knew it was unlikely that all members of this extended family would all be together again in one place, and certainly never again in Richmond.

When Biggie planned all this, she had no idea just how important this reunion would be for me and my children. While Deb and I were flying to Richmond, my parents rented a car and drove two and a half hours south into North Carolina to pick up my children from their mother's home and bring them to Richmond. We stayed together in a borrowed apartment across the street from Biggie's home, held on to each other for three days, and took long walks through the quiet streets of Biggie's neighbourhood.

When we joined the extended family in Biggie's house, I lost myself in conversations with cousins I hadn't seen in many years, devouring mountains of food delivered by her vast network of Richmond relatives and friends. The one thing you can count on in the South when there is some kind of family misfortune is deliveries of food, roasted meat in particular. My mother has rejected many Southern traditions, but she always holds a ham in reserve for times of trouble. There have been days when I called my mom in some kind of crisis and she would arrive at my door within hours with a large cooked ham cooling in a cardboard box. As we consumed roasted meat that fall in Biggie's house in Richmond, we gazed at the portraits of our ancestors and felt the presence of ghosts all around us.

We buried Biggie beside her husband, Walter Williams, in Hollywood Cemetery, a vast garden estate beside the James River. She first met Walter beside a mailbox on a street near Monument Avenue on a sultry summer evening when they both happened to be mailing letters at the same time. He was wearing a tuxedo because he had just come from a party. Biggie was smitten, and so was he. Biggie told me this story many times when I was a boy and liked to show me the spot on the very street corner where they met.

He had died years earlier, having suffered from Parkinson's disease in the final years of his life.

Biggie nursed her husband when he was sick and after he died, picked herself up and went on living in the most determined way imaginable. She travelled the world, came often to Canada, and even flew to Newfoundland when we were living there to see her great-grandchildren. When she arrived, she encountered a skeptical two-year-old Gabby. If you don't have a middle daughter, I suggest you borrow one from time to time to keep your ego in check. Gabby has been calling me on my shortcomings even before she was able to speak. As a toddler, she would look me up and down with her all-knowing, bemused brown eyes and then walk away. That day, Biggie received the silent once-over and said, using one of her old Virginia expressions, "I think she finds me wanting."

"Yes," I replied, "she does. She finds me wanting too."

I have no way of knowing this for certain, but I think Biggie was trying to tell us something about life and loss when she transformed her death, our loss, into a grand family party. Before we dispersed the morning after her funeral, we all posed for a family portrait on the front steps of her house. When I look at that photograph, I can almost hear Biggie's voice, telling us to look at ourselves there on her porch. We are still breathing the air. Pause long enough for the shutter to click and then get on with living.

Gabby came home to New Brunswick the Christmas after Biggie's funeral and made plans to finish her high school studies in Fredericton. And so in our bungalow on the outskirts of the city we became three. We fell into new routines, and my daily telephone calls were now to Danielle and Aaron, and I helped them with their homework assignments by email. Gabby continued to tell me the story of her days, only now she was perched on a stool by the kitchen counter, keeping me entertained while I cooked dinner.

11

Danielle returned to New Brunswick after her high school graduation and moved into an apartment in the city with friends, with plans to attend university in the fall. Aaron planned to stay with his mother and return to us during the Christmas and summer vacations. The first summer he returned, the summer after Biggie's funeral, when Aaron was thirteen, was the first time we went to the lake.

A few days before he was scheduled to return to North Carolina, we decided to go camping, just the two of us. We tossed some gear in the back of the Toyota, drove to Saint John to pick up my father's aluminum boat and motor, and continued driving south toward the United States border. Our destination was Spednic Lake Provincial Park, which is situated near McAdam, New Brunswick, a railroad town that has fallen on hard times in recent years. When the national railways pulled out of McAdam, the economic engine of the town went with them. The once bustling railway yard just north of the border is now silent and overgrown with weeds, while the big trucks rumble along interstates farther north.

We stopped in McAdam to fill the cooler with ice and groceries and to pick up some fishing supplies. We repacked in the parking lot, turned back on the road, and drove slowly through the town, passing boarded-up store windows on the main drag and the majestic red-brick railway station on the hill, still advertising a lunch counter that had stopped serving meals long ago. When I pass through these forgotten places on the east coast, I feel as if I've drifted into the margins of a page, that the stories told here are outside our society's main narrative. That morning it felt just fine to be out there in the margins; another few miles and we would disappear off the page altogether.

We turned off the pavement onto rutted dirt roads that took us to a provincial park that has also fallen on hard times. The campground and boat launch were built with government money that employed some people from the town after the railways left. When the grants dried up because the park enterprise didn't make sense on some bureaucrat's balance sheet, the camping facilities and walking trails were left to crumble and decay and slowly return to the New Brunswick wilderness.

The New Brunswick and Maine border runs through Spednic Lake, a sprawling, shallow, rocky network of bays, springs, and creeks that forms the source of the St. Croix River, which becomes the international border farther south. The border runs through the middle of the lake, an invisible line that snakes over and around a maze of rocky islands, so when you're out on the water you're floating in a kind of no man's land, an international aquatic grey area, one minute in Canada, the next in the United States.

The park was deserted when we arrived that morning. We drove to the concrete launch pad and floating wooden dock, backed the trailer down into the water, and unhooked the boat from the winch. The boat immediately started to sink because we forgot to screw in the drain plug. But Aaron managed to plug her before she went down, and we got good and wet and had a big laugh while we bailed the boat and loaded our gear. The lake was flat calm. The sun was rising over the treeline, shimmering out beyond the dock, which was still in shade. The water felt soft and warm and had that earthy smell about it, that sweet summer lake smell of dirt and moss and leaves that gets in your nose and coats your skin. I parked the Toyota on the edge of the woods and walked back to the boat. Aaron sat waiting in the stern. The stillness of the lake and the big sky was all around us. I sat in the front of the boat and poled out from the dock with an oar. Aaron flipped the choke and started the motor and eased us out into the lake.

As soon as Aaron was old enough to operate a fishing rod, my father decided he would try to make his oldest grandson a real fisherman. He found Aaron a small pair of women's hip waders that were still several sizes too big for a little boy, outfitted him with a short spinning rod, and took him bushwhacking through alder thickets and mosquito-infested bogs to his secret brook trout streams, where he taught his grandson early that real fishermen must endure a certain level of hardship before they find sweet pools of cold swirling water that hold big trout. When they had their fill of stream fishing, they spent days on lakes, trolling for smallmouth bass and landlocked salmon. In my father's little aluminum boat, Aaron learned how to be patient and take part in boat conversations, during which the most serious problems of fishing and world politics are always addressed.

When Aaron had paid his dues on trout streams and lakes, my father bought him a little Browning trout fly rod and took him to the Miramichi and Restigouche rivers, where Aaron began to fly fish for Atlantic salmon. Aaron learned to cast and hook and land these big fish in big water with his little rod, and as he grew older and graduated to full-sized gear, he developed the kind of smooth and natural casting motion that can't be taught in fly fishing schools.

My father's fishing school had a make-or-break curriculum. The early bushwhacking experience would have turned most small boys off fishing for life. Aaron refused to be broken and came to understand that we find grace in this life in small moments, and that, as Norman Maclean tells us, "all good things — trout as well as eternal salvation — come by grace and grace comes by art and art does not come easy."

In the course of all these fishing trials and tribulations, Aaron learned to handle an outboard motor better than anyone in our family, and he developed a solid sense of direction in the wilderness, so he was in charge of running the boat and finding a camping spot as we crossed Spednic Lake and followed the American shore away from the park. We watched the swells from our wake fan out until they lapped against the beach. All signs of our passage vanished behind us in the morning sunlight.

We were searching for a camping place on an island, and we found some promising sites where we stopped and explored. But we were in no hurry to unpack the boat, so we decided to keep looking until we found a place that felt right. When we arrived at Palfrey Neck, we knew we were there. Palfrey Lake is at the northern end of the Spednic Lake system. The camping place we found was not on an island, although for us it might as well have been. Our site was on the end of long, narrow peninsula at the entrance to Palfrey Lake. We were surrounded on three sides by water and on the fourth side by miles of wilderness.

Some years ago, the park work crews expanded the camping facilities out into the lake, floating picnic tables out to some islands and to places like Palfrey Neck. They cleared spaces for tents and built outhouses without the house — just a small privacy screen on one side and the forest and big sky on all others. Someone had constructed a deep fire pit with lake stones and fashioned a lookout seat from notched ash boughs so we could sit and lean against a tree beside the shore. There was a nice breeze blowing across the open spaces on the point to keep the flies down, a small beach for landing the boat, and deep water for swimming.

We pitched the tent and tossed our sleeping bags and gear inside, slapped together some sandwiches, and then headed back out onto the lake. Aaron stayed at the tiller the whole trip. We had an agenda of nothing. We fished for bass, but didn't work at it too hard. Aaron wasn't interested in fishing himself, because an experienced fisherman can catch a co-operative smallmouth bass pretty much anytime he wants, and he'd been there and done that many times, but he put me onto some nice bass among the giant rocks along the shoreline. The fish jumped and ran, and we released them back into the lake. When we got tired of that, because even fishing felt like too structured an activity, we motored out into deeper water where we didn't have to worry about knocking the propeller off on a boulder hidden just below the surface.

We went swimming whenever we felt like it. Aaron, like a true thirteen-year-old, felt like it every ten minutes or so. We swam all over the lake, just dropped the anchor and jumped out of the boat. Our favourite place was a deep cove on the Maine side where there was no wind but lots of sun. We dove off the boat and listened to the sound of our voices echoing off the hills. Back at Palfrey Neck, we swam under the moonlight and then warmed ourselves by the campfire and played cards by flashlight. I remember thinking as we toured around the lake during those two days that my son had become my guide on this trip, that our roles had been gently reversed, and that perhaps he was going to continue to be my guide through this phase of our lives together.

We laughed a lot and never spoke of difficult things, although there were many difficult things we could have discussed. Our summer time together was coming to an end, so we were carrying around a big hurt in our chests, knowing that he was going to have to leave when we returned home. Our third morning we ate the last of our bacon and eggs and broke camp. Two days later, he was packing to go back to North Carolina.

The night before he left, I dreamed I was hiking along a rocky ocean shoreline. I was on a spiritual quest, travelling with friends, exchanging books, and stopping for long talks. Waves were crashing against the cliffs, the pathways were narrow, and the footing, treacherous. By the end of the journey, I had come to a new understanding about the fragile course of our lives. At least that's how it appeared in my dream. My new understanding was this: the things which are, are beautiful. I had fallen asleep reading *The Things Which Are*, a collection of poems by Alden Nowlan, and his words had been shaken and stirred in my dream. Nowlan had found his title in John the Apostle's account of the purpose of his writing in the book of Revelation: "Therefore write the things which you have seen, and the things which are, and the things which will take place after these things."

All of this made sense to me, including John's journalistic mission statement, until I woke up and spoke the words out loud and they fell flat at my feet, the way epiphanies in dreams so often collapse in the moments after we open our eyes. The things which are, are beautiful. Good grief. That wasn't going to take me very far.

Nevertheless, I told Aaron and Deb about the dream as I drove to the airport in the early morning darkness, and they mumbled some sleepy words of encouragement, having listened to me strike out on such strange tangents before. Then Aaron boarded his plane and I wept while Deb drove us home.

12

That winter, Deb and I decided to get married. We had broached the subject of marriage with mixed feelings. Like most girls, when Deb was young she had played bride, imagining herself walking down the aisle in a long white dress. Then as a teenager, she had watched her parents divorce and the parents of her friends divorce, and she had decided that she would never marry. Who in their right mind would will that kind of misery on themselves? During the six years she lived in a common-law relationship, she had refused to make it official by getting married. During the dark year, I had also told myself that I was through with marriage, and that if I managed to make a life with someone else the institution of marriage wouldn't be part of that union. However, now that we were living in a common-law partnership we wanted to hold some kind of ceremony to mark the promise we were making to each other. The more we talked about it, the more we recognized that it was the traditional wedding ceremony that was turning us away from marriage.

My first wedding was traditional in every respect, with the bride in a white dress, and the bridesmaids in matching dresses, the men in rented tuxedoes and shiny black shoes, and me nursing a nagging hangover from the obligatory boys' night out the evening before. My brother and sister had similar weddings, with rehearsal dinners, and string quartets and dinners and dancing, all of which made for lovely family parties but with the hindsight of a trio of divorces just seemed like a terrible waste of money. The grand wedding is a remarkable holdover of a tradition that has endured despite the inherent instability of today's marriages.

We wanted to leave all this behind and focus on the choice we were making to be with each other. We did not want to be distracted by seating arrangements and song selections and spending thousands of dollars on a ritual we knew had nothing to do with living love as a verb.

As we struggled to come up with a wedding plan we could embrace, we needed to put aside our ambivalent feelings about marriage for one purely practical purpose: we needed to get married because we were planning to adopt a child. Since the beginning of our relationship, we had spoken of Deb's longing to have a child and about my own reluctance to father another child.

In part, I had what I considered to be purely selfish feelings — that I had survived many years of parenting and wanted to experience adult life without the responsibility of young children. I wanted the freedom to travel the world and take more river trips and do the kinds of things that I had such difficulty making a priority when my children were young. I loved being a dad and raising my children, but I had been through the worrisome years and didn't want to go back. That was part of my internal struggle. The fundamental struggle was more difficult to articulate.

The fallout of my divorce had caused my children to leave before I was ready for them to leave. In particular, I had watched my boy leave, my baby, and while my girls had returned, he was still living most of each year far away from me. I had experienced gut-wrenching pain, and I didn't want to risk feeling it again. What if something happened to our child? Or what if something happened to us and we split up?

All the while I struggled with my reservations, I knew I had to consider Deb's desires. One evening, I told her I had been wrestling with all of this and didn't think I could overcome my fears of having another child. She collapsed on our bed and wept, big, full-body sobs, and said that she had never imagined her life without raising a child of her own. I knew that this was a test of our love. Was I willing to extend myself for her, so she could be all she could be? If Deb needed this, and I was going to continue to make a life with her and ask her to make a life with me, how could I deny her most fundamental need?

For a long time, I struggled with these questions, and was unable to overcome my reservations. Then one day when we were driving home from a visit to her family in Halifax, Deb started talking about a story she had produced when she was a reporter for CBC television several years earlier, about a couple named David Jewett and Diane Nadeau, who had adopted two baby girls from China. The two little girls were beautiful, happy, and well adjusted, spoke both English and French (their mother is francophone), were learning to speak Mandarin, and were adored by their parents. In the course of her research for the story, Deb had learned that there were thousands of baby girls in Chinese orphanages, waiting to be adopted. Most of these girls had been abandoned by their parents because of China's one-child population control policy. Many rural Chinese parents cannot afford to keep a second daughter. These farm families, ruled by grandparents, prefer boys, who will stay at home and work the family farm when they become men. Tradition dictates that girls marry and move away to work on their husband's family's farm.

Deb confessed that international adoption had always been her backup plan for having a child in her thirties, that as her twenties passed without finding either a life partner or a potential father for her child, she fantasized about travelling to China to bring one of those little girls home. She wondered what I thought about the idea. We began a new conversation that afternoon in the car and continued it when we came home. The more we talked, the more I felt we could undertake this journey together. Some choices we make in life can't be explained rationally. They just feel right in your gut.

During the following days and weeks, we talked about travelling to China to find a daughter. We could raise a child who also needed us. Perhaps there was a child already in the world who was waiting for us to love her. Deb and I had found love on the road of second chances. Perhaps there was a little girl waiting for a second chance in a new family. This child would join our family by choice, not biology. If we found her, and she found us, this would be a child we would love, and all of the members of our complicated and extended family could love, not because of a biological imperative, but because we had chosen to bring her into our lives, and she, by being in the particular place she was at this particular time, had chosen to be with us. We decided to set out together to find our daughter.

Deb started researching the adoption process. She called Dave Jewett and Diane Nadeau and told them of our plans. They invited us over for a brunch with a gathering of families who had adopted in China. Dave is sweet natured and gregarious and considers their two journeys to China to adopt their daughters the most profound moments of his life. Since his return to New Brunswick, he has done everything possible to stay connected to China, including becoming the first non-Chinese president of the local Chinese Cultural Association. He encouraged and reassured us and welcomed us into this network of families who had adopted daughters in China. Diane told us about their trips to China, and how their second daughter was sick with a terrible abscess on her head when they arrived and how she had simply said to herself, "I don't know what we need to do here, but we are going to have to do something." They found a doctor in China and began treatments that continued back in Canada and ended with the little girl's complete recovery. Both Dave and Diane promised to be there for us through the adoption process whenever we needed them.

One of the first things Deb discovered in her research was that if we were going to adopt a child in China, we needed to get married. At that time, the Chinese government would allow single men and women to adopt, but unmarried couples were not welcome. So although we had planned to get married anyway, now we had a reason to make it happen sooner. We set a date and made plans for an unconventional wedding. We wanted only a handful of witnesses at the ceremony. Therefore, we needed to keep the event a secret from our families and friends until after it had happened. We would get married and then call everyone and give them the news.

One Friday morning in February, Deb and I woke up and dressed for a wedding. Deb wore a purple lace dress with a matching jacket. I wore my grey Saks Fifth Avenue jacket that I had found in a second-hand store and had had tailored to fit, and a red bow tie given to me years ago by my uncle, who believed real men should know how to tie bow ties. About a half an hour before we were due at the church, we drove to town, stopping at a flower shop on the way to pick up a boutonniere and a bride's bouquet, my only surprise for Deb that morning.

We arrived at St. Anne's Chapel-of-Ease, a hundred-and-fifty-year-old stone chapel connected to the more modern Anglican church in downtown Fredericton. Barry Craig had recommended St. Anne's as the perfect setting for a small wedding. When I approached Barry and asked him if he would perform the wedding, he hesitated. He told me he was going through a separation from his wife and that he would understand if under the circumstances we wanted to find someone else. I told him that we asked him to perform the wedding because we wanted him, that regardless of what was going on in his life we still held him in high regard. I also took the opportunity to tell him that if he ever needed someone to talk to about what he was going through, I was available, although most of what I knew about separation and divorce and parenting children through these difficult times had been learned through my own mistakes.

Our decision to be married in a church, by an Anglican priest, did create problems, but they had nothing to do with Barry. I always teased Deb about her unconventional religious beliefs, or lack thereof. She is a spiritual person who embraces the values of the Christian ethic, including the radical idea of loving our neighbours as ourselves. She just doesn't buy into the whole son-of-God story. I told her that in my Presbyterian world it was an all-or-nothing proposition. My father, a very open-minded clergyman, is accepting of the many religions of the world. He was perhaps the most ecumenical of all the ministers in our hometown, accepted and respected by Catholics and Jews and Muslims alike, but when it came to what Presbyterians must believe, he was absolutely firm that there were limits. Deb wanted a wedding ceremony that made no mention of Jesus or God, a request that my father would have responded to by suggesting we find another minister to perform the service or, more appropriately under the circumstances, a justice of the peace or a licensed operator of an Elvis wedding chapel in Las Vegas. In fact, my father had performed so many marriages that had such tenuous connections to the church that he had long ago reached the conclusion that he would prefer to get out of the wedding business altogether.

Barry agreed to Deb's request out of friendship, perhaps against his better judgment, and perhaps because he was at a time in his life when all of his presuppositions about marriage were being challenged. He agreed that he could write a wedding liturgy that would contain what he believed was the necessary spiritual component of a wedding ceremony without any specific reference to the Christian Church. We thanked him for making this generous compromise.

The wedding party consisted of Barry, Walter and his new partner Melinda, Gabby, and a friend who took photographs. I had telephoned Danielle and Aaron the night before and told them we were getting married. They were the only ones who knew about the event in advance. Barry composed a lovely talk about the nature of love and how love allows us to help our partner be all they can be in this world and in the process we become more of who we are. He spoke of the capacity of two people to will what is good for each other. We said our vows, written with Barry's help, which were a combination of traditional language and words we wanted to say.

One of the traditional lines we took out was the promise that we would love each other till death do us part. Deb told me she thought this was an unreasonable expectation, and I agreed. We hoped that our love would endure throughout our lives, but we knew that it depended on us caring for it and nurturing it every day, regardless of any promises we made in the chapel one morning in February. In the end, we found words that we thought expressed the spirit of the day and our partnership, and although it was still our secret, a suggestion of the great adventure we had in mind for ourselves to travel to China to adopt a child.

Barry pronounced us husband and wife, and after we signed the papers to make it official, we all drove to a local hotel where we had reserved a table for a celebratory lunch. After lunch, we made a series of telephone calls from a pay phone in the lobby to tell our parents and other family members that we had got married that morning and would be back in touch about plans for a summer family party and celebration. Gabby went home with my brother for the weekend, and we drove across the border into Maine.

We had loaded our ski gear in the back of the car before we left for the wedding that morning. A few hours down the road, when we stopped for gas, we changed out of our wedding clothes in the bathroom at a gas station. Late that evening, we arrived at a bed and breakfast in Rangley, Maine, near the Saddleback ski hill. It was icy cold and there were mountains of snow in the yard. The next morning we had breakfast early and drove to the ski hill. For two days we skied during the day and ate leisurely dinners and drank bottles of wine in small restaurants in Rangley in the evenings, soaked our tired bodies in a huge claw-foot bathtub, and went to bed early. We skied until our legs would no longer safely support us, and then we packed for home. When we returned, Gabby came back from Walter's house, and we all fell back into our routines.

That summer, we invited our families and friends to our home for the weekend to celebrate our marriage. We set up tables in the yard under the shade trees. We bought two roasting pigs from a farmer, who recommended we hire a friend of his who had come to New Brunswick from Bosnia, to roast them for us. I woke up early on the morning of the party to find the man in our yard with a blazing fire and the two pigs dressed on a spit. When I asked him if he would like me to bring him a coffee, he requested a beer, so I went inside and poured him one and refilled my coffee cup and sat on the lawn for the next hour or so, watching the meat sizzle and sputter over the fire, listening to the story of his flight to Canada when war came to his city in Bosnia. He and his wife and children had been forced to abandon their home in the middle of the night with nothing but what they could carry, had flown as refugees to Fredericton and since then had been doing everything they could to restart their lives from scratch. He had been working two jobs and learning English, trying to save enough money to buy a house and return his family to the standard of living they had left behind.

Later in the day, the crowd of family and friends arrived. An exuberant Tim Nobes commandeered a plastic garbage can full of beer and organized a softball game in the park down the street. It was a summer celebration of love and family and second chances. The last of the guests drifted away at sunset and we were left in the quiet evening together to wash the dishes and bring in the folding tables and chairs and congratulate each other for throwing a good party. That evening, I told Deb the story of the man who had roasted the pigs, and thought to myself that I was the most fortunate of men and that if I ever complained about what I didn't have, I need only remember that quiet man who had lost it all and was still able to find the strength to start again.

14

One of the gifts of a second chance in love is that we can learn how to make love and how to foster intimacy in a relationship. True intimacy is a coming together of *eros* and *philia* in a place that is safe and free and allows for the fullest reciprocity in kindness and generosity. In an intimate relationship, the opportunities for growth and discovery of each other are infinite. There is pleasure in familiarity and pleasure in the knowledge that over time we will keep moving into places we have not been before.

The great truth most men will never acknowledge is that when we were young and vital, with flat stomachs and tight bodies filled with testosterone, we were terrible lovers. We were terrible lovers because we didn't understand what women need, and we didn't recognize the connection between making love and intimacy. What we learn, if we are open to learning, is simple. It's not about us. All of us who want a happy love relationship with a woman should consider becoming a student of the female orgasm. When we look after our lover and give her what she needs as many times as she needs it, we will receive in turn what we need.

A comedian once said that unlocking the female orgasm is like typing on a computer keyboard, searching for the password. If you actually stumble upon it, the next time you go back to the keyboard the password has changed and, in fact, the keyboard is using a different script altogether. I recommend reading the many excellent books out there with information about the female orgasm — we need all the help we can get.

Over the years, I have learned that giving a woman what she needs begins outside the bedroom. For example, if your lover appreciates a clean and orderly household (and it is a safe bet that many woman and men do), cleaning the house from top to bottom, including scrubbing bathrooms, makes a person more attractive. Every time I hear complaints from women that they are doing all the household chores, I figure I may also be hearing a sad story about a man who, through his own neglect, is missing out on more than a clean house. Cooking a gourmet dinner, lighting candles, and opening fine wine may help set the mood, but your partner may be thinking more about who's going to be washing the dishes when the meal is over. Wining and dining is for boys. Real men get out the scrub brushes and the cleaners and the mop and wear their rubber gloves for a few hours on a Saturday morning, and in the process, engage in foreplay on an entirely different level. I recommend cleaning the oven, changing the burner guards on the stove, and mopping the kitchen floor. Wash and dry the sheets, remake the bed. Then you can get ready to mess it up again.

I maintain there is a hockey metaphor for every moment in life, and here in our part of the world, we use them all the time: the colleague who can (or can't) put the puck in the net, the co-worker who needs to learn to pass the puck or needs to be sent to the penalty box. The hockey metaphor can even extend into the bedroom, at least when we consider the way Wayne Gretzky, the greatest player in the history of the game, approached hockey.

Gretzky was born with wonderful natural talent, but he was never the strongest player or fastest skater or hardest shooter on the ice. His game was all about his attention to detail. On game day, he made the most of his time. He would be the first on the ice and the last to leave the ice during his pre-game warm-up. Sometimes he would be skating hard, but often he would be just shooting the puck, not blasting it at the net, but flipping it on his stick, tossing soft shots up against a post or the crossbar, looking for new angles and new approaches to the net. When the Zamboni came out to flood the ice, he would reluctantly return to the dressing room to regroup while waiting for the game to begin in earnest.

Once the game was on, Gretzky rarely tried to do everything himself. He communicated with his teammates and became the greatest passer in hockey history. He'd carry the puck if he saw open ice, but his game was all about passing and his ability to see the action unfolding before him, to sense where the play was going before it moved in that direction. His genius was his ability to take those extra few seconds, hold the puck, wait for the open man, then at the perfect moment pass the puck to a teammate who would put it in the back of the net.

I watched Gretzky often on *Hockey Night in Canada* broadcasts. Lesser players, usually younger players, don't have his kind of patience. They try to force a goal when they are too far out or don't have a clear shooting lane. The next thing they know, the whistle blows and they're sitting on the bench, scoring opportunity lost, waiting for another shift. When you're in the lovemaking game, think about the Great One, holding that puck, just holding it there, waiting for an opening.

The beauty of this game is there's no time limit for a career and few physical limitations. It doesn't require grand athletic prowess, but attention to the tiniest details, in soft, slow, almost imperceptible movements. It's about discovering the true nature of *eros* and *philia*, and about giving and receiving in kind. It gets better with age. In the world of second chances, we have the opportunity to learn to be real players. This is one of life's great gifts indeed.

15

In the weeks that followed the wedding, Barry took me up on the offer to talk. We met in a downtown pub for a beer, and he told me that his marriage had fallen apart, he was in love with another woman, and he didn't know what to do. He had started to realize something was wrong when he was working in his office on campus the morning after Christmas. His friend and colleague Sara MacDonald had come to pick up a gift she had left in her office one floor down, had seen his car in the parking lot, and had stopped in to see what was up.

Sara is a professor of political philosophy who grew up in the Miramichi River valley in New Brunswick. She returned to her home province and St. Thomas University after she completed her doctorate at Fordham University in New York. When she arrived at St. Thomas, she and Barry became close friends and taught classes together in the Great Books program. When she found Barry working in his office that Boxing Day, she asked him what he was doing working through the Christmas holidays when his wife and three children were at home. Barry told her that he was a busy man with many important commitments and that he needed to come to the office every day of the week and most evenings to meet them. She left with her gift and went home, and he stayed in his office, no longer really working but thinking about what had happened to his life and wondering whether maybe something was wrong.

Over the next few weeks, he decided that his work schedule was excessive. Moreover, he admitted to himself that he was profoundly unhappy, not really "excellent" at all, and that he wanted out of his marriage. He wanted out but didn't know how to go about it. As an Anglican priest, he had always understood that marriage was for life. He was increasingly miserable. Then he recognized that what he really wanted was to spend more time with Sara, which made him even more nervous and frightened.

In time, he told his wife he wanted to end their marriage and that he was attracted to someone else. Sometime after that he decided he had better tell Sara what was going on. They had developed a daily ritual of walking down the hill through the campus pathways to the university library to pick up books. As he told me his story, I recalled how I used to watch them pass by my office window, walking together, deep in animated conversation, often laughing, completely absorbed by each other's company. Barry, still outfitted in his buttoned-down attire, walked with his shoulders hunched over, his hands in his pockets. Sara was usually in high heels, her long reddish blond hair blowing in the wind, her blue eyes flashing over at Barry before she burst into laughter at something he said.

Sara later told me about a day when they were walking back up the hill from the library, when she felt Barry's hand awkwardly clutching her shoulder. "There's something I have to tell you," he croaked. She said her first instinct was to run away. They stopped walking and she waited for him to speak. He told her he had fallen in love with her, at which point they decided to extend the walk. She told Barry that she was inclined to like him a little too. Then their troubles began in earnest. Sara had been married for two years to her high school sweetheart, whom she had dated for sixteen years. In the months that followed, Barry and Sara suffered heartbreak and grief in the process of formally ending their marriages, while the gossip percolated through the campus. Some of Barry's colleagues urged him not to have a relationship with Sara and told him he was ruining his life and destroying his reputation.

Barry felt as if he were carrying a million pounds of bricks on his shoulders. He told me about his intolerable burden that night in the downtown pub. He felt he had to go back to his wife and make the marriage work, although he wanted to be with Sara. He had spent fifteen years counselling couples to stay together through the good times and the bad, and he believed that he had to be an example for his congregation, that he had to live a life of absolute probity. He thought that he had let down his congregation and that people were disappointed in him. I had little advice for him other than to tell him that people would be interested in his troubles today and someone else's troubles tomorrow.

Meanwhile, Sara was doing what she had trained her whole adult life to do: to think her way through the problem. She decided that the difficulty for Barry, and their friends and colleagues who cast harsh judgment on them, is that their version of a life of virtue didn't allow for the pursuit of happiness. In teaching Aristotle and contemplating the ancient account of virtue, Sara had come to the conclusion that our goal as humans is to be as happy as we can be. In the opening lines of his *Nichomachean Ethics*, Aristotle suggests that happiness, *eudaimonia*, is the highest end in human life. This is not a hedonistic life of pleasure seeking but a life lived in accordance with our understanding of virtue or excellence, the English translation of the untranslatable Greek word *arête*. The *Ethics* is an exploration of the virtues that help us find happiness in this life, virtues that for Aristotle include generosity, temperance, prudence, and wisdom. Happiness is not a state of being, but an activity, a way of living. Aristotle defines happiness as "an activity in accord with virtue."

Barry continued to struggle because, as an Anglican priest, he couldn't get past what he had been taught, that marriage is a sacrament and is supposed to be for life. Sara told him that people are not meant to be unhappy. If the prerequisite for a virtuous life was to stay married, how could something that was making him so unhappy be good or right?

Jean Vanier notes that the idea of the pursuit of happiness is often accompanied by guilt: Why do I have the right to pursue my own happiness when other people are suffering? Vanier concludes that Aristotle has faith in human nature. "If in every human being there is a desire for happiness, then happiness is possible," he writes. "Nature is not an evil genius that makes us see some inaccessible mirage. Nature is good. It does nothing in vain. Just as the seed planted in the ground unfailingly yields flowers and then fruit, so human beings can progress to happiness – not unfailingly in their case, but providing they identify it, seek it, make good choices, and understand that its attainment may take a lifetime."

Of course, we can think our way through all of this and believe we have made it out of Dante's dark woods and up the side of the mountain — then we realize nothing is as easy in practice as it is in theory. Sara moved out of the house she shared with her husband and bought a falling-down house across town, where she hoped she and the man she wanted to love would make a home. Barry moved in with Sara, stayed for a few agonizing weeks, and then, unable to bear the weight of his guilt, returned to his wife.

Eventually, Barry came back to Sara and stayed. The human capacity for forgiveness, to recognize, accept, and forgive the failings of those you love, allowed Sara to open her door when Barry came back. She understood that we have to be able to forgive our partners when they don't live up to our standard of virtue, as we need our partners to forgive us when we fail.

"I wanted to live a virtuous life," Barry told me years later during a long conversation in his office. "For me, it was a question of trying to figure out what the shortest path to virtue was. And I had come to the conclusion that the shortest path to virtue was to be with Sara. That anything other than that would have just been a life without any integrity at all, just lying and pretending to be in love with someone and wanting to be with somebody else. For me, in the end, it had to be that, even though one priest I talked to said,

'Well, it looks to me like you've concocted a very clever rationale to excuse your sin.' In the end, I realized that trying to explain to the world what I was doing was kind of a foolish enterprise."

He came to recognize that he had a kind of crazy pride or arrogance associated with love, and that he had been trying to show the world how great his capacity was to stay married and weather the storms — just as he had counselled couples to do for all those years. He decided that this pride was in fact leading him away from an authentic Christian account of virtue.

According to the teachings of St. Paul, we are saved not by our good works but by grace. In the apostle's radical new account of the nature of the virtuous life, salvation is based on the grace of God, not on our ability to follow the laws of the church to the letter or to live a strict life of virtue in the Aristotelian model. In other words, we live a good life in its most complete sense, and we are forgiven for our essential fallibility as human beings.

Barry realized that until his marriage fell apart, he was proud of how he had managed to stay in this relationship and be faithful. When he returned to Sara, he understood how imperfect and, therefore, how truly human he was and how dependent he was on grace and forgiveness, not just from God but from Sara too. He truly understood the nature of grace only when Sara forgave him and loved him when he came back. He was no longer a man who believed that he should be loved for all of his virtues. "For me it was coming to understand God's grace to us," Barry said. "But then the other side is having that same grace in our dealings with other people, to be just as forgiving as we are forgiven. This isn't a conditional forgiveness. God doesn't say, I forgive you but I am always going to remember it."

He also came to believe that the crisis in his life offered him a rare opportunity for spiritual growth and an understanding of the possibilities of a happy life, which he had never had before.

Although I didn't know it when I asked Barry to perform our wedding, he later told me that for years he had refused to remarry people who had been divorced. When he was a priest in Blackville, no divorced person had ever been remarried in the parish during the one hundred and forty years before he came, so he maintained the rigid standard. By the time he moved to Fredericton, he had started to soften his position and to reconsider his understanding of how God's grace works in the world. Sometimes we mess things up and sometimes we are redeemed. We nonetheless go forward as best as we can. Sometimes we can't live with our spouses. If we are able to find a new marriage that makes us happy, why wouldn't that be a good thing? Grace is about being offered second chances.

Barry found himself wishing he could redo his years of providing marriage counselling. He had come to a new understanding of the weakness and frailty of people and how some of the things he had asked his parishioners to do in their unhappy marriages were beyond what they were capable of doing. He also recalled times when he had learned of various scandals involving the private lives of other members of the clergy. He recalled, in particular, how a married priest had fallen in love with another woman, and he had been one of the ones spreading the gossip and passing judgment about the man's decision to pursue a love affair. When his own marriage collapsed and he and Sara made their relationship public, he felt terrible about his condemnation of that man's actions.

As their turmoil and troubles receded and the gossips moved on to more current subjects, Barry and Sara finalized their divorces and got married. They began making a life together, searching for common ground beyond the intellectual life they shared at the university. Barry introduced Sara to his greatest passion in life, the Boston Red Sox. I would run into them on campus early in the fall semester, both red-eyed from lack of sleep, having just driven all night from a baseball game eight hours south in Boston. When they first began making a life together, she thought this was a passion of his that they had to share in its complete sense. Then one summer after she had been on two guided tours of Fenway Park in Boston, she realized that she had her limits. They could be together, and she would watch the occasional baseball game, but her love for Barry would not include sharing in his obsession with the Red Sox. They have found a middle ground, about baseball and other passions in their lives. Sara is a morning runner; Barry hates to exercise. These days I often see them together in the mornings on campus walking back from the athletic centre, Sara flushed from a morning workout, Barry clutching a coffee, never having broken a sweat, carrying her books and gym gear.

"If we live in the little hovel we live in now till we retire it won't touch at the core of what makes us happy," Sara told me one morning. "There are things we would love to do if we had money, which we don't at all. But by the same token, if we never had more than we have now, we know we are capable of having a perfectly happy and wonderful and fulfilled life, such that I wouldn't risk any of it for a million dollars. Life is short, marriage can be short, we're going to go out and have a lot of fun."

Barry now considers his marriage to be the best and most important part of his life. He now works only when he needs to and longs to be with Sara and at home with his children when they are with him. He still enjoys his university work, but he doesn't put it ahead of the family. "What I want more than anything now is time, more time, all the time I can have with Sara," he told me. "Looking back on it now, the only regret now is that I wasn't with Sara sooner, and I didn't act much faster when I realized how important she was to me."

16

The next summer, Aaron and I planned a trip back to the lake and the island, even though we knew it couldn't be the same. We wanted to visit that magic place again, and Aaron wanted to show Deb where we had been. In the end, we returned with a group: Deb, Walter, his partner, her son, and his cousin. Aaron brought his guitar wrapped in garbage bags, and we had two boats and more tents and mountains of food. My brother was in an expansive frame of mind, fully in the moment, trying to fish and swim, eat and drink beer, and supervise the raising of an enormous tarp over the picnic area in case of rain, all at the same time, from the moment we arrived at the campsite. We spent one night at Palfrey Neck. The water level in the lake was lower and the weather was colder and rainy, but we swam and cooked over an open fire and passed around the guitar until the early morning hours when we stumbled off to our tents in the darkness, promising to return to the lake and Palfrey Neck again.

Aaron was a foot taller that summer, and he had let his hair grow long and shaggy. Once again we had six weeks, and he guided us through it. One afternoon a few days after he left, I found myself heartsick with missing him, thinking about the lake, and life's losses, and Henry Thoreau. Thoreau is widely misunderstood as a kind of hermit who lived in the woods beside Walden Pond. He did live in a cabin beside the pond for a couple of years, but he was no back-to-the-land pioneer, for his cabin was situated only a few miles from town, and he was back and forth almost every week. When he arrived in the woods and began to clear a spot for his cabin, he wasn't making a political or ecological statement. Rather, he was searching for a way to cope with intense inner pain.

He was twenty-eight years old, had failed as a teacher, and was working to become a writer but was having difficulty finding publishers. He had fallen in love with a woman who rejected him. Then his older brother, the person he loved most in the world, had died, and Thoreau had almost died himself, his grief was so profound. He had made friends with Ralph Waldo Emerson, had been hired to tutor the philosopher's son, and then Emerson's son died. As a capstone event in this string of misfortunes, Thoreau went fishing outside his hometown of Concord, Massachusetts, lit a fire to cook the catch of the day, and burned down a huge tract of woodland. Some people in Concord blamed him for not seeking help quickly enough. Susan Cheever notes in *American Bloomsbury*, her account of the life and work of Thoreau and Emerson and the other writers in his New England circle, that the local newspaper, the *Concord Freeman*, wrote that Thoreau was "thoughtless and careless" and bore responsibility for the fire.

"He had seemingly lost everything — his beloved brother, the only woman he ever loved, the prospect of a literary career, and the prospect of a teaching career," Cheever writes. "Now his work could begin." So he went to the woods, perhaps as a way to make restitution to the forest and natural spaces, and, carrying a burden of grief, built a little cabin with his own hands, lived there for two years, and emerged with a remarkable, beautifully crafted long essay in which he concludes that too many of us are living lives of quiet desperation. He argues that we must have an end that transcends our obsessions about our economic well-being and all of the factitious cares of daily living. He wrote that we have become obsessed with matters external to the best part of us. Our highest virtue, he says, should be to affect the quality of a day.

Walden Pond helped to advance Thoreau on his spiritual journey, but it didn't take him to the end. He makes it clear that he never intended *Walden* to be a how-to-live-better book. He never returned to Walden Pond to stay, although for the rest of his life he often visited wild places. So what was going on down there in the cabin beside the pond? He offers us these perplexing lines: "I long ago lost a hound, a bay horse and a turtle-dove, and am still on their trail. Many are the travelers I have spoken concerning them, describing their tracks and what calls they answered to. I have met one or two who had heard the hound, and the tramp of the horse, and even seen the dove disappear behind a cloud, and they seemed as anxious to recover them as if they had lost them themselves."

Thoreau scholars have written many pages trying to explain this allegory, because the author's own explanation of the passage leaves us wanting more. "I guess we've all had our losses," he once replied when asked about these lines. You have to admire old Henry and his tenacity for tossing out an answer like that. But, of course, this is really the point.

In fact, Thoreau is jumping up and down trying to wake us up. His allegory is about indescribable inner losses, which can only be expressed through poetic images like the hound, the bay horse, and the turtle-dove. He uses these images because our losses are specific to each of us, and when we accept them for what they are, we can find friends on the trail, people who are searching too, and help each other along the way.

When Aaron returned to North Carolina, my depression returned. Deb and I needed to start the social worker's study that would allow us to begin the adoption process. I told Deb I wasn't ready to make the first appointment. I couldn't articulate the reasons why, I just wanted the process to stop until I felt I was ready. Deb was furious, but for days I refused to discuss the matter further. Finally one night, I started talking and the conversation continued long into the night. We reached the conclusion that I was holding on to the pain of Aaron leaving. I didn't want to let it go because it was all I had of him. How could I love him as much as I did, and then lose his presence in my life, and still go on to pursue happiness in my life? What if I actually found myself happy without him? How could I be a happy man if I didn't have my boy in my life? I had to say it, and name it, and then I was able to begin to let it go. That night I wept, the same hard tears I wept the first day he left, and the next morning, I decided it was time to get on with the business of living. I could hold him close to my heart without holding on to the pain. The way to find happiness required a letting go of the sadness.

Years later, I realized that evening I had remembered the lessons of the lake and of Henry Thoreau. We've all had our losses. But we all have a hard time accepting them in a world where the prevailing mythos is that we must strive to win at all costs. Governments divide societies into the haves and the have-nots, writing some stories on the main page and scribbling others in the margins. No politician has ever won a campaign preaching the gospel of life's necessary losses. According to the mythos, the people who really know how to live never admit they've lost anything.

Our inability to face our losses creates dire consequences. We start popping pills in an attempt to dull the pain. When marriages end, we use the word failure, and the courts choose winners and losers; one wins the television, the other loses the stereo, one parent wins custody and the other parent is awarded visits as a consolation prize. We admire nothing more than stories about snatching victory from the jaws of defeat. But is this not a mythos built on a foundation of smoke and mirrors? How can this be a life where we are all winners in the end?

If I were to follow the formula of the mythos, this is where I would say that I lost something when my son left but found something else that is more wonderful, something that I wouldn't have found if he hadn't left. In that version of the story, Aaron and I both win, and in that victory we find happiness. That's the Hollywood ending that's so trite and so false that it makes me angry enough to spit. No, the losses have been real and deep, and when I cut through all of the rationalizations, I can't think of one goddamn good thing to say about them.

But on the first trip my son and I took to Palfrey Neck, we felt the presence of grace all around us, and we allowed the desperation, anger, bitterness, and loss to dissolve in the sweet waters of the lake. My boy showed me that we didn't need to always speak of what we were losing, that we would find a way through this, a way that involved letting the pain go as best we could. In the years to come, we would speak of it when we needed to; the rest of the time we would just hold on tight and ride it out. We had been bestowed grace in abundance. We dove deep, emerged from the water, pushed our heads up into the sunlight, understanding that the things which are, are beautiful indeed.

Making for Home

1

The journey to China to find our daughter began the day we met Dorothy Frazier. The first step in seeking approval from the New Brunswick government to adopt a child is to arrange for a social worker to conduct a home study. We discovered that Dorothy, a social worker who had helped some of our new friends adopt from China, lived in our neighbourhood. She had recently retired from the New Brunswick civil service but was still conducting home studies and offering counselling as a freelance consultant. Deb and I had agreed that neither one of us was going to be a silent, passive partner in the big moments of our life together. I was the one who had been filled with angst about beginning the adoption process, so I was the one who picked up the telephone to ask Dorothy if she would work with us and to set up our first meeting in the following week.

I was ready to move forward with the adoption, but I was constructing various fearful scenarios in my mind as we waited for Dorothy to arrive that evening. Deb kept telling me this was just the first step in a process and that we would pass through it just fine, but I was worried. My experience with social workers and family psychologists had all been in the context of a divorce, when the professionals I encountered were searching for weaknesses in one parent or the other, or problems in one household or the other, pointing out more often what was wrong than what was right.

We opened our front door to find a curvy black woman with short-cropped hair, a huge smile, designer eyeglasses, and gold bracelets. We invited her in, and she settled herself on a straight-backed chair by the front window of the living room and asked for tea. Our first meeting was a short session to get acquainted and to make a plan to get the work done.

Despite the fact that she was smiling at me and trying to laugh at my jokes, I was still nervous as hell and trying hard not to show it as I served the tea. Dorothy outlined her plan to conduct a series of as many as eight visits before she would write her report. The first stage of the process, she explained, was the completion of a genogram of our family. A genogram is like a family tree, but a family tree with substance, a diagram that explores relationships. The lines in a family tree are straight, the corners are square, and the turns are all right angles. The lines in a genogram are not always straight. Some are curved, others are broken. Nothing is written in black and white. Dorothy told us she would be bringing her coloured markers.

When she returned a couple of weeks later, it was late November. The three of us sat around the little table in our breakfast nook and began a long conversation about love and families that Deb and I continued long after Dorothy had left us. In the beginning, it was difficult for a couple of journalists to sit quietly and answer questions. We had many questions of our own, although Dorothy was tough to crack. More than once, she gently reminded us that she was the one who needed to ask the questions. Nonetheless, over time, we discovered that Dorothy had a remarkable story and that we had invited into our lives a person who was eminently qualified to determine whether we were a suitable family to adopt a child, and, in particular, to adopt a child of another race. We also recognized early on that Dorothy was far more interested in building us up than tearing us down. She believed in our ability to overcome obstacles, perhaps because she had overcome so many of her own.

Dorothy was born in Little Rock, Arkansas. Like all cities in the Jim Crow South, Little Rock had segregated stores and restaurants, bus station waiting rooms and lunch counters, public washrooms and drinking fountains, and, of course, schools. In 1954, when the U.S. Supreme Court ruled in the *Brown v. Board of Education* case and declared segregated schools unconstitutional and the NAACP began trying to enrol black students in schools throughout the South, a school board in Little Rock agreed to admit black students. In the fall of 1957, nine black students, specially selected for their maturity and academic excellence, were enrolled at Central High School in Little Rock. Dorothy's best friend, Carlotta Walls, was one of the group that became known as the Little Rock Nine. The story that unfolded that year in Little Rock was arguably the seminal moment in the non-violent civil rights movement.

The segregationist Arkansas governor, Orval Faubus, deployed the state National Guard to stop the students from entering the school, and in September 1957, the guardsmen and an angry mob of whites did just that. The NAACP went to court to ask for protection for the black students, and it asked the federal government to enforce the ruling of the Supreme Court. The stage had been set for a legal and moral showdown.

President Dwight Eisenhower sent in federal troops and federalized the Arkansas National Guard. The nine entered the school with an armed escort, and the soldiers remained with them for the rest of the school year. Because of her relationship with Carlotta, Dorothy was close to much of this turmoil. During the 1957 school year, Dorothy's mother, along with other parents whose children were considered academically suitable, was meeting with NAACP leaders about what would happen the following year. Dorothy was a strong and confident girl, an excellent student, and a fine candidate to be part of the second wave of black students to enter Central High. There were some concerns she might be too hot-headed, but Dorothy's mother decided her daughter should attend Central High School the following year, and Dorothy agreed to go. Then at the end of the school year, Governor Faubus played the last card in his hand and closed all the high schools in Little Rock rather than integrate them. So instead of entering Central High, Dorothy went away to a boarding school in North Carolina.

After graduating from high school, she attended a liberal arts college in Vermont and then joined the Peace Corps because she wanted to travel in Africa. She lived and worked in Nigeria and Uganda, and along the way, married a white man, a decision that was unthinkable in the world of her youth but was not uncommon among the young people who were immersed during their formative years in the vision of the non-violent movement. Four of the Little Rock Nine married white partners and went on to have biracial families. They married for love and walked the talk of colour-blindness throughout their lives. When Dorothy and her husband settled in Fredericton, she joined the province's civil service, where she worked with families as a social worker and then as an adoption specialist until she retired.

During our conversations, we discovered that Dorothy harboured no bitterness about the world of her youth. It seems that sometimes when people witness humans at their worst they are able to walk away from this experience to be more forgiving of the sins of others than those of us who regard these events from a distance and wonder how all of this could have happened.

"I don't see colour," Dorothy said when I asked her about how this experience changed her view of the world. "I see people. If there is prejudice, I don't see actions as prejudicial. I just say, 'People aren't thinking.' I haven't let my childhood experience colour how I see the world. People have to show me that they are unworthy of my trust."

All of this became part of our conversation with Dorothy during the early weeks of that winter as she prepared our family's genogram. Deb and I sat on one side of the table and watched her spread out a large sheet of newsprint and neatly arrange her coloured markers beside it. Then she folded the sheet in half, ran her hand down the crease, paused to take a sip of her tea, and said, "Who wants to go first?" I volunteered.

Dorothy had learned how to develop genograms more than two decades earlier when she was working on her degree in guidance and counselling. She first used them as a method of helping young people relate to their own families, to show them how little they knew about their own stories. During the process, they would start to ask questions of their family members to try to piece together who they were. They discovered that they knew their parents and they knew their grandparents, but they never thought about who they themselves were and how they interacted as children, and how close and how distant they were from particular family members.

When she started doing home studies for adoptions, she always began with a genogram. Among other things, it was an excellent ice-breaker, a way of getting the partners talking and listening to stories about their own lives. The person who is listening learns a lot he or she didn't know, or interjects and adds to the story that the other is telling. "It's a matter of finding out how your families operated," she told us. "And then, when I put you together, how do you operate?"

I told her about my grandfather who bought the old house and about Gan-Gan, and Biggie and her husband, Walter Williams, and about my family's journey from the southern United States to Canada. She drew little boxes for each of these characters and made notes about each member of the family beside the boxes.

Beside my father's box she wrote: "Retired Presbyterian minister, Harvard Divinity School grad. Disciplined kids when young. Involved in the Civil Rights Movement. Great role model. Philip maintains connections to organized religion because of Dad." Beside my mother's box, she wrote: "Highly educated. Teacher. Stayed home with kids till they graduated high school. Ran writing centre at the University of New Brunswick till mandatory retirement. Activist. Involved parent. Has incredible energy and drive." She noted that my mom comes from the Carter family, one of the old Virginia aristocratic families. I remember Dorothy smiling and saying a soft schoolyard "oooh" as she took out her red marker and wrote "The 'Carters' of Va." on the newsprint, letting us know that she both knew what this meant and was unimpressed by my family pedigree. She made notes about my parents' relationship: "Shared parenting. Shared 'power.' Love story. Together (no secrets). Argued but always made up."

She noted that I was close to all my siblings, and that my sister Sadie was a stay-at-home mom in Nashville (she drew a long curved line to my sister's namesake, our great-grandmother Sadie on my father's side). She placed Susan in Ottawa, teaching at Carleton University when she wasn't travelling the world. She drew a broken line to my sister's former husband. She noted that Walter was living in Saint John, coaching hockey, working at the university, with a new woman in his life who had a son, whom Walter was now step-parenting. She drew a dotted line from this boy to his biological father, who was also now connected to our lives. She drew a broken line to Walter's former wife. The picture was taking shape.

Then she drew my box. She noted that I was forty years old, and she drew a dotted broken line to my former wife and solid lines to Danielle, Gabby, and Aaron. I told her about my first marriage and my three children, and how my son was living with his mom in North Carolina and that Dorothy would be able to interview him during the Christmas holidays. All the way through the process, Dorothy interrupted with questions: "What do you think about when you think of your mother? What kind of a person was she?

What about your dad? Who was the disciplinarian? How did they do it?"

She made notes about how I had made rules in the house when I was a single dad: "Look after yourself. Tell us where you are and what you're doing. Be reasonable about curfew. Be polite. Don't take anger out on others. Respect." She made some notes about my relationship with Deb. She wrote at the top of the sheet: "Work at it." The word *work* is circled and underlined. She also noted: "Deb describes Philip as an idealist."

Several visits later, Dorothy announced that she was through with me and she turned the paper over and started drawing Deb's genogram. Now I was able to sit back and listen to the stories of her family, some of which were new to me.

Deb told Dorothy the story of her family's origins in the city of Montreal. Deb's mother, Susan, has the maiden name Leroux, which can be traced back to two brothers who came to Canada during the seventeenth century as part of "Le Regiment de Carignan" to fight the Iroquois in the Indian Wars. One of the brothers, who went by the nickname LeCavalier, married a woman named Marie Renaud, who was one of "les filles du roi," a group of women who were sent by the king of France to the New World to become the wives of French soldiers.

One of Deb's great-grandfathers on her mother's side was an Irishman named Moore, who had boarded a ship to see some friends off, had a few too many drinks, and woke up in the midst of an Atlantic crossing. He landed at Pier 21 in Halifax and eventually settled in Montreal, where he found work as a plasterer. He brought his wife over from England and in the course of their marriage, they had sixteen pregnancies. Nine of the children lived into adulthood.

Deb's parents met in Montreal at the church where Susan's dad was caretaker. Tim Nobes was the son of the owner of a men's clothing store in Montreal, but the Nobes family roots are on the East Coast, in Nova Scotia. Tim and Susan married young. Deb's memories from her early childhood are of her parents being happy together and affectionate and supportive. They knew how to laugh and they knew how to have fun together.

The marriage began to unravel as her dad's construction business grew and he began working long hours away from home. She told the story of how when her parents separated, her dad moved across town with her brother, Brendan, and she stayed home with her mother. Brendan's box on the newsprint noted how he, too, was in the construction industry and that he was always patient with and protective of his little sister. Dorothy drew a dotted line to Deb's childhood friend Michelle, who was so close she had become an addendum to the family.

She made a box for Deb's dad. Beside it she wrote: "Supportive. Made efforts to be part of Deb's life after separation and divorce." Beside the box for Deb's mom, she wrote: "Legal secretary. Was a homemaker. She was also a foster mother. Emergency home for foster care system." I had heard these stories before but never in this much detail, about how as a child Deb would wake up and walk into the kitchen and there would be a strange boy or girl sitting at the table eating breakfast, or a malnourished baby in her mother's arms that had arrived in the night. The children would stay there until they returned to their biological family or were moved to a more permanent home.

Both of Deb's parents remarried. Deb has a stepsister and stepbrother on her father's side. She has made lasting friendships with both of them. Susan also married a second time, to a retired navy man, who has children and several grandchildren, which meant more boxes and more solid and dotted lines. Most of the extended family on Deb's side live within a short drive from one another's homes in Nova Scotia. Beside Deb's box, Dorothy wrote: "Friendly. Self-confident. Outgoing. Felt celebrated as a child." She drew a line to a little girl whom Deb had brought into our lives during a time when she was volunteering for the Big Brothers Big Sisters program.

Then one day Dorothy arrived and announced that it was time to join us so we could see the complete picture of this modern family. She unfolded the paper and spread it out on the table. She selected a green marker and drew a line between my box and Deb's box. She put the cap on the green marker, uncapped a black one, and wrote along the line: "Lived together from 2001. Married 2003." We spent that session admiring the portrait of a family. There were relationships of all kinds, of blood and of friendship, half a dozen divorces and the same number of second marriages. Dorothy started asking us what we had learned from the process. What did we take from this? What did we learn about marriage from our parents? How much of their experience had we incorporated into the relationship that we have? She told us that we would have taken up some things and discarded others, especially the parts that we believed were dysfunctional. We needed to continuously reflect on what we value in a marriage. However, she reminded us that we always take things from our parents, whether we like it or not.

When Aaron came home for Christmas, I told him he needed to be interviewed by Dorothy for the home study. She had already interviewed Gabby, and since Danielle had moved to an apartment in the city, she didn't need to be part of the home study. Aaron did, because he was still a member of the household, even if he was away for part of each year. Dorothy dropped by the house one afternoon between Christmas and New Year's, and he sat across from her at the kitchen table with his ball cap pulled down over his eyes and answered all her questions in monosyllables and shrugs. What did he think about having a new sister? Shrug. Was he excited, nervous, angry? Double shrug. Did he just not care? Nod in the affirmative. I watched this unfold with a sense of dread as I puttered about the kitchen. I figured Dorothy would have some hard questions for me about what kind of parent I had been to raise such a sullen creature. At our next meeting, I was preparing to tell her how lovely Aaron really is and how the boy she saw the other day is not the real him when Dorothy plunked herself down in her usual chair and announced that he was a sweet boy who played his role as a young teenager to perfection. She was letting me know everything was just fine, that she had been there and knew what she was dealing with.

By then we understood that this home study was not just a screening to make sure we were suitable to adopt a child, but also a preparation for the adoption, to make sure we were communicating with each other so that we would be able to turn to the adoption and all its challenges as a team. We talked about how marriage is a partnership, about how we tried to run the household as partners, and how raising this new child would be a shared responsibility, and that our daughter would be coming to both parents equally for nurturing. We made plans to share a year of parental leave when our daughter came home with us from China to start us off on this kind of equal footing.

Dorothy always seemed to turn the conversation toward our strengths. She told us she wanted to help us discover our strengths because we were going to need them when we began this new phase in our lives. We all have weaknesses, and they are right in front of us most of the time. We also all have strengths, but it helps to be reminded of them. We also found strengths in unexpected places.

She pointed out that the splits and divisions in our families, all the new additions outside the traditional bonds of blood and first marriages, could be seen as strengths, not a trail of broken promises and failures. We were a family that was accepting of new people and new kinds of relationships. Deb's mother loved and cared for foster children. Deb grew up in a household that was accepting of many different types of love relationships, including step-parents and step-siblings and friends who were invited into the family circle. Deb's life story involved making family connections that were outside traditional blood lines. Now I was also part of that story.

Early in the New Year, we received our report from Dorothy. She recommended that we be allowed to adopt a child. She reminded us in the report that we had a lot going for us. "There are many strong points in the Lee/Nobes marriage that include (1) they genuinely enjoy each other's company and love to spend time together and have lots of fun together when they do; (2) they have a very strong bond that allowed them to listen to each other and communicate openly and settle differences through discussion and negotiation; (3) they love to make each other laugh; (4) they are very physically and verbally affectionate with each other; (5) they are supportive of each other's personal and professional accomplishments; (6) they love and appreciate each other for who they are and don't have any intention of trying to change each other; (7) they have a profound friendship and deep spiritual connection; and last, but not least, (8) they love each other in the active sense of the word love." That would be love as a verb.

She observed that I appreciate Deb's good humour, optimism, and sharp mind, and that I admire her sense of adventure and her ability to give herself over to the moment. She wrote that Deb appreciates my patience, my "unflagging confidence" in the people I love, my ability to listen to her and make her laugh. She noted that we have fights (we tried not to have too many when Dorothy was in the room) but that we try to resolve our differences through discussion, negotiation, and compromise. We always forgive each other in the end, unconditionally. She noted that being a step-parent has been difficult for Deb, and that at times we have disagreed about how to resolve issues related to the children. However, we were both learning how to parent teenagers together.

What Dorothy had given us was not a critique of our marriage. Her report cast no judgments about the complicated makeup of our families. As far as Dorothy was concerned, this was all just interesting and meant that our little girl could be loved by more grandparents, and a larger pool of friends and relations. It was certainly the most encouraging document we could have received.

2

We filed Dorothy's report with the New Brunswick government and received a letter in return that it had received the report and concurred that we were a suitable family to adopt a child. Then we began to work through an Ottawa-based non-profit agency called Children's Bridge to complete the final stage of the adoption. Dave Jewett and Diane Nadeau had worked through Children's Bridge, as had most of the rest of the families in our city who had adopted internationally. We knew Children's Bridge had coordinated several hundred adoptions from China for Canadian families and had an experienced staff that understood Chinese bureaucracy and had deep connections in Asia. Children's Bridge received our file from New Brunswick and arranged for it to be translated into Mandarin so it could be sent to the China Center of Adoption Affairs. In the spring, our file was sent to China. The agency told us to be prepared to wait up to a year to be matched with a child and to be notified of our time to travel. The file included Dorothy's report, letters from each of us about why we wanted to adopt a child, photographs of us and our home, and copies of medical examinations and tax returns. Bureaucrats at the China Center of Adoption Affairs in Beijing would review our file to make sure it was complete and then at some point transfer it to "the matching room."

From time to time, a photograph of the matching room will circulate on the Internet. However, for the most part, what happens in the matching room is a closely guarded secret. I always wondered what kind of strange magic runs through this small corner of China's sprawling bureaucracy. How do these people, whom we have never met, whom we will never meet, find our children for us among the hundreds of faces they are presented each day? We have heard various stories about how the matching is done, that among other things the matching room staff search for physical similarities in the photographs of prospective parents and children, although surely this can't be the guiding principle when they are looking at photographs of infant Asian babies and adult western parents. Most of the information they have about the character of the babies was gathered when they were less than a year old, so the suggestion that they are matching for personality traits is also wishful thinking.

All we knew was that at some point our file would reach this room, and one day during the course of some man's or woman's workday, our file would be opened and someone would put us together with the daughter who was meant to be ours.

The Greek poet Sophocles was fascinated with these kinds of movements, and named this mysterious moving force in the world fate. Sophocles composed his most famous tragedies using the myth of Oedipus to explore how much of our life is preordained by fate and how fate and free human action are related to the stories of our lives. If I were to apply the Greek understanding of fate to our adoption story, I would say that we had made the choice to adopt a girl, and yet this little girl was somehow already meant to be ours, even before she was born. The Oedipus story fascinated Sophocles because of its extremes. Oedipus was a man who was fated to kill his father and marry his mother, and when his fate was revealed at his birth by a blind seer, his parents decided that their infant child should be put out in the countryside to die of exposure. His feet were bound and he was hung from the branch of a tree. This was their attempt to thwart the movements of fate. However, the infant boy was rescued by a herdsman, who named him Oedipus, or "swollen feet," and raised him as one of his own. Oedipus, like all of us, was blind to his fate. When he was a young man, Oedipus killed a man in self-defence after an argument while travelling on the road to Thebes, and when he arrived in the city, he married the man's widow. Just like that, one bad road trip, and he killed his father and married his mother.

In my studies of Greek poetry, I was always fascinated by what happened to Oedipus. The usual end for a tragic hero such as Oedipus is death. But instead, when his crimes are revealed to him, Oedipus blinds himself and is destined to wander the Greek world as a transient, outside of the associations of humans. He reappears in what I consider Sophocles's greatest play, *Oedipus at Colonus*, where we find him an old man, making peace with his daughters before his death. Oedipus's blindness has turned him into a blind seer, and he is able to see the world and the movements of fate more clearly than those who possess the physical ability to see. Oedipus accepted the lot that was given him and is transformed into a man of exquisite beauty and wisdom. Oedipus wanders with his daughters, Antigone and Ismene, into the village of Colonus, a holy place on the outskirts of Athens. There, Oedipus is made a citizen of Athens by Theseus, the king. Before he dies, he tells his daughters: "You had love from me as from no other man alive."

We all struggle in our blindness. We are free to make choices, but when we understand that our destiny is not always in our own hands, we can find some measure of peace in the world. The way I see it, we make the best choices we can make and recognize that we are also caught up in the mysterious and powerful movements of fate. The final peace that Oedipus reaches at Colonus comes from his understanding of both the freedom and limitations in human life.

3

During the time when we were waiting for our file to make it through the matching room, Deb and I spoke often of the movements of fate, and for long periods, we found ourselves surprisingly calm. Everything would happen when it happened. The circle would come around. We decided to trust our agency and make the most of the time we had before the baby arrived and changed our lives forever. Since we had been together, we had almost always been busy with children and various crises in our lives. Gabby was still at home but was busy with her own life and independent, so we had a period of freedom to do what we wanted to do most of the time. We wanted to live as large as we could while we had the chance. So whenever we had free time we went out to the movies or to the theatre, or out for dinner. On Saturday mornings we fell into a routine where I would make a pot of coffee, bring a cup to Deb, and then we would go back to bed and stay there, lost in the quiet spaces of our own little world until late morning.

During the winter, we spent weekend afternoons skiing at our local hill. In March, we both took a week off work and rented a small condominium at Sugarloaf Mountain in northern Maine. We skied every day until we were too tired to ski any more, then retired to the hot tubs and swimming pool and sauna, cooked dinners, and collapsed exhausted into bed.

When spring came, we started biking on the weekends on the network of trails in the city, stopping to drink beer on patios, and browsing in used clothing stores for baby clothes. I made friends with the grandmothers who were rummaging through the clothing bins and learned how to exchange items by publicly declaring who we were shopping for. I told the ladies that I was shopping for my daughter, and then I would explain that I hadn't met her yet but I expected she would wear clothes suitable for a small twelve-month-old girl, the age that we expected our daughter would be when we received her in China.

We also started renovating the house. I moved out of my office and into Deb's office. The shared workspace took some getting used to, mainly because I am a mess of a worker, leaving books and papers piled high on my desk, and Deb is a neat worker who files away every piece of paper at the end of the day. We painted the bedroom that had been my office in a light violet. We hung new curtains in the window and Deb's mom bought us a white wooden crib that we assembled and made up with new soft sheets. We moved Deb's childhood dresser into the room. Downstairs, we converted one of the three bedrooms into a mudroom for the dogs so we could isolate them from the rest of the house when we needed some peace. We started the process of getting rid of things we didn't need, including piles of junk from my previous home that I had moved into the basement in boxes and never touched. I held several free yard sales and watched my stuff disappear from the side of the road. Every time some more of my things disappeared from the curb, I felt liberated, that I was simplifying my life and focusing more on the things that mattered, which had nothing to do with the accumulation of material things.

We recognized that our system of collecting receipts in a cookie tin and settling accounts at the end of the month was a good system for maintaining our financial independence in the short term, but it was impractical and unnecessarily time-consuming. We negotiated a system whereby we would open a joint bank account and each contribute money for shared expenses. We kept separate bank accounts and credit cards. We continued to always try to deal with money issues in a businesslike fashion and not to allow emotion to become linked to financial discussions, especially when we were preparing to spend thousands of dollars on a journey to China.

As each week passed, we were thinking more and more about our baby. Deb wrote in her journal: "I wonder if she's even been born, whether she has a name, who her parents are. If she hasn't made her way by now, then she will soon — and I wonder if her mother has decided yet what to do. How random this is — it seems so strange that one mother's decision to abandon her daughter, a decision likely not yet made, will make a mother out of me. I am waiting for my daughter. I prepare every day, walking around in the rooms of my mind, examining all the piles left in corners, folding and putting away, dusting and preparing a clean and loving place for her to occupy. I see little girls everywhere. I wonder every day what she will look like. She will come so far to be with us and I know we will be ready."

That summer we received word that that the processing of files was moving much more quickly than expected at the China Center of Adoption Affairs. In fact, if the pace continued, we might be matched in the fall and travel early in the New Year. Deb made note of this news in her journal and added: "She has definitely been born." About this time, Aaron arrived home for the summer and we spent a long and lazy weekend at the old house, exploring the beaches, swimming in the icy waters of the bay, and playing guitar on the front porch. "Aaron is home," Deb wrote in her journal. "He is so beautiful I can hardly stand it."

Late in the summer, about a week before Aaron left to return to North Carolina, Deb's old lady dog became ill. She had been slowing down for a couple of months, and when we found her that evening lying on the floor and unable to walk, we called a veterinarian who was on call that night and arranged to meet him at his clinic. I carried Riz to the car, and Deb held her in the back seat.

By the time we arrived at the clinic, Riz was dead. Gabby, who had come with us, wept with Deb in the parking lot over that old dog that had driven all of us to distraction since the day she moved in. With her usual practical wisdom, Gabby told Deb that Riz was in a place where every day was garbage day and where everybody always leaves the top off the garbage can. This made Deb laugh through her tears, and then she handed the vet the body of the friend she had raised from puppy to old woman, and he carried the remains of old Riz inside the clinic. The vet would arrange for her cremation, and we would pick up her ashes later in the week. Deb called in sick the next morning and went to bed for a couple of days.

In time, we began to imagine that old Riz had, in fact, been needed elsewhere, that, as strange as it sounds, perhaps she had been sent to China to watch over our new daughter, wherever she was. "I asked my old black dog to be as loyal to this baby as she was to me — and to stay with her for as long as it took for us to get there," Deb wrote one day in her journal. "Maybe that's crazy but it helps me to think of her there. Maybe that's why she left us."

During the waiting period, we continued to make connections with the New Brunswick families who had adopted in China. We went to dinner parties at Dave and Diane's home, and every time a new baby came home from China, we went to the airport to join the welcoming party, which always consisted of a pack of little girls who had themselves been adopted in China. The first faces the new baby girls saw upon arrival in this strange new land was a crowd of little girls who looked like them, who reached out to touch their new "cousin," to stroke her hair or rub her cheek and then run back into the arms of their own parents.

On one of our trips to the airport, I stood beside Dave on the side of the arrival area, admiring the gaggle of girls running in circles at the airport, and I remarked on how precocious and beautiful they all were. He replied that we shouldn't forget that these girls were the strong ones, who had survived abandonment and a year or so in an institution, and who had been healthy and strong enough to get themselves noticed when orphanage officials were making adoption lists. He said they were remarkable children, indeed, and how fortunate were we that they had come into our lives.

That fall we attended the Harvest Jazz and Blues Festival, a three-day city party with acts staged in tents erected in public spaces in downtown Fredericton. When I left home the first night out, I was wearing my pager to keep in touch with Gabby, who was really too old to need to reach me at any moment. I was in a habit of wearing the pager and I felt undressed, and somehow derelict in my duties as a parent, if I left it at home. That night, somewhere on the streets of Fredericton, the plastic clip broke and the pager was gone. When I discovered that it was missing, I started to retrace my steps to locate it in the dark, and then I decided it was one of those things that was meant to happen. I probably could have found it, but I just stopped looking. Instead, I threw the plastic clip into a garbage can and went back into the tent to hear some more music. I was moving into a new phase of my life, and I no longer needed to be on constant call. Soon enough I would be answering a baby's cries in the night, and I didn't need a pager for that.

4

As we navigated the adoption bureaucracies, it helped that Deb and I had worked so long as journalists We had spent most of our professional lives dealing with bureaucrats and government officials during the writing and production of stories. We understood the rigid nature of bureaucracies and knew that following the process to the letter was critical. We also knew that, while rules needed to be followed, if for some reason we didn't get everything exactly right the first time, we'd get there one way or another.

We ignored the rumours circulating on Internet adoption chat rooms and listened to the professionals at our agency, and, therefore, were able to predict the day in November when our referral might arrive from China. It was a Friday, and Deb took the day off work to be home when we got the word. That afternoon, Deb took the call in the kitchen and took reporter's notes and asked reporter's questions. We were told our daughter's name was Cen Xiao Ru. She had been born on January 27, 2004 — my birthday. Surely that had helped to bring us together. Somewhere in the matching room in Beijing a bureaucrat had seen the two dates and decided we fit.

Our daughter had been born somewhere in rural China on my forty-first birthday. During the first week of her life, her parents had abandoned her in a place where she would be found, in the city of Heng Feng in Jiangxi Province in south-central China. Cen Xiao Ru was living in the Heng Feng Social Welfare Institute.

We knew she had spent the first ten months of her life in the institution. The fact that, unlike many of the girls, she had not been sent to foster care likely meant that she was healthy and strong, as it was often girls needing special attention who were cared for by elderly couples in the town. We searched the Internet for information about Heng Feng and found photographs of the orphanage. We even discovered a Yahoo group of families who had adopted children from Heng Feng. We joined the group and started an email dialogue with people from around the world who had been there before us. We stared at the photographs of the Welfare Institute's buildings online, the arched gate and garden in the front and the motel-like barracks on either side, one section for children, the other for elderly people who also needed to be cared for. This was her home on the far side of the world.

On Monday, we knew our daughter's file had arrived with our provincial bureaucrats in Fredericton and that it included more detailed health information and photographs of little Cen Xiao Ru. We wanted to see the file as soon as possible. This was the only moment in the process when we lost our cool. When we called the New Brunswick adoption office to arrange to pick up our file, we were told that we would have to wait several days because the information had to be given to us during a meeting with a social worker who could help us to determine if this was the appropriate child for us. This person would be a social worker who up to this point had had no involvement with our case. Moreover, we were informed that this particular employee was on a training course. We were also told we would have to wait because this department's priority was the welfare of "New Brunswick children." Well, that was the wrong message to send to a couple who had been waiting patiently for months and who could recognize a bureaucratic brush-off a mile away. We could accept the rules — so long as they made some small amount of sense. I started working the phones, climbing my way up the chain of command in the Family Services Department. Meanwhile, Deb called in a favour from a staff member in the premier's office who made some calls to the director of adoption services in New Brunswick. Our daughter was from China, but she was a New Brunswick child.

By the end of that long day, we had arranged for a meeting early the next morning. When we arrived at an office on the north side of the river, we met with a social worker accompanied by her supervisor. As we sat in the office signing forms, we realized that our file was incomplete and was a photocopy of the original. We asked her where the original was, and eventually located it in another office on the south side of the river. We drove across the river to the downtown office and by mid-morning finally had our daughter's file and photographs in our hands.

The three photographs had been taken three months earlier. In one of them, little Cen Xiao Ru was dressed in flannel pyjamas that were several sizes too large. She was sitting in a blue high chair staring at the camera with a furrowed brow and what appeared to us to be a face filled with worries. What was she worried about? Was it the stranger with the camera? Was it that her nannies had told her that this photograph was going to be sent to her mommy and daddy and she was worrying about who we were and whether we would come for her? Could she understand anything about what was happening to her, about what was about to happen to her when we arrived in China? The black fringe of hair she had had at birth was receding. She had delicate features, lovely little lips, and long fingers. Her eyes were rich and dark. We decided at that moment, sitting in the reception area of the government office, that we had never laid eyes on a more beautiful child. We forgot all about our frustrations with the process.

We walked out onto the street holding the file and photograph of our daughter. It was a windy November afternoon, and as we walked to our car we saw Dave Jewett crossing King Street holding two takeout coffees on his way back to the office. We called his name and waved him back to the sidewalk. He knew the moment he saw the smiles on our faces that we had our referral in hand. Dave fussed over the photograph, told us how beautiful she was, pumped our hands and congratulated us, and reminded us again that he had told us that when the time came we would be matched with the daughter who was meant to be ours. While we were talking to Dave, we turned around and saw Sara MacDonald walking past us on her way to run errands downtown, and received more congratulations.

As we drove home, we noted how remarkable it was that our daughter's file had come all the way from China, and that we had spent the morning bouncing from office to office in our little city and that at the very moment we walked out into the sunshine we had bumped into the man who had inspired our adoption journey. I had never encountered Dave on a coffee run in that place before and never have since. In this world, we can either believe in fate and magic, or not. As we moved closer to Cen Xiao Ru, there was no question which side of the fence we were on.

5

We would travel to China in six weeks and would be there for two and a half weeks. We would spend four days in Shanghai in the south, and then travel northwest to Jiangxi Province to receive Xiao Ru. We would spend a week there, and then travel north to Beijing, where we would spend another week completing immigration paperwork before flying home. The relaxed part of the waiting period was over. Now it was all worries and agonizing over the details of the trip. We visited friends who had just returned home with their third daughter from China. They gave us some of the practical things we needed for the trip, such as money belts and zip-lock bags of medicines, and they helped us to make lists of things to bring. We bought new luggage and baby supplies. About this time, I started worrying about what Cen Xiao Ru would eat. What kind of bottles and nipples did we need? What kind of baby formula should we bring? Would she eat rice cereal? Part of the problem was that we didn't know what she had been eating in the orphanage. But I was also unable to remember anything about feeding a child of her age. I figured I had this information somewhere in my mind, but for the life of me I couldn't retrieve it. I was disappointed with myself. I had been a parent of small children before, but I feared I would not be able to remember enough to do it right the second time around.

Deb had been shopping for months preparing for the trip, and many times she asked me what we would need. I kept telling her I couldn't really remember. Then, usually in the evenings when we were sitting in our daughter's room, which had become the packing room, something would hit me in a flash. And I would say something like, Where are the receiving blankets? You know we'll need those to put over our shoulders when we're burping her and she spits up. And what about a plastic diaper change pad? We've got one of those, right? And Deb would write these things down on her shopping list, casting a slightly pained look in my direction, letting me know she was happy to have a veteran parent on her team but that she wished he was just a little more on top of things.

6

Somehow we made it through Christmas. Aaron returned to us for a couple of weeks, but I remember little else about our family celebrations. The teenagers were coming and going, and acting their age. One evening after they had all banged out the door and the house was finally quiet for the first time in days, I said to Deb, "At least we're not adopting a teenager."

That Christmas, our friend Jen Beckley gave us a quilt she had made for Cen Xiao Ru. The quilt was an irregular work of brilliant reds, an auspicious colour in China, and bits of cloth in a rainbow of colours she had gathered from many sources. When she brought it to our home on Christmas Day, it still needed to be finished and was held together with pins. She promised to finish it while we were away and told us we could wrap our daughter in the quilt when we returned.

We were thinking all the time about the trip we would make a week after New Year's. Deb made Christmas cards with Xiao Ru's referral photograph on them, and we made one paper tree ornament with her photograph pasted on it and hung it on our tree. I don't remember what I gave anyone for Christmas that year, but I do remember writing a poem that I stuffed in Deb's stocking. It was inspired in a strange way by a rather indulgent Oliver Stone football movie called *Any Given Sunday*, which we had watched as part of an Al Pacino theme movie weekend (we were ranging around for anything in those days to distract us from the endless trip planning). Pacino plays a troubled football coach, and as flawed as the film may be, it has what is surely one of the great locker room scenes in the history of sports films. It begins with a haggard-looking Pacino pacing back and forth, trying to rally his team at halftime. It's a variation of the "life is a game of inches" talk, but at that moment, I bought in, as if I were in the locker room and Pacino was addressing me.

The locker room speech is over the top. And there is nothing original in the cliché that life is a game of inches. But when I watched the speech for the first time, I knew that for many years I hadn't been paying attention to "the six inches in front of my face," the phrase Pacino uses as the anchor of his speech. And for the most part, day in and day out, that's where the game is played. We fight for that inch, and then we surrender to the hands of fate. And I knew that our daughter was in that orphanage in Heng Feng just doing what she needed to do to survive, day in and day out, until we arrived to take her home. So I wrote a poem for our new daughter, inspired by this crazy football movie, gave it the title "Waiting for Xiao Ru," and put it in Deb's stocking.

Living is
The six inches in front of your face.
Every minute. Every second.
Al Pacino taught us this.

These days
We're stumbling and tripping
With our eyes fixed
Half a world away.

Falling apart
And falling back together again,
Dreaming deep
Mysterious China dreams.

Xiao Ru
We dream of you.
Dark eyes and little hands
Living one inch at a time.

I remember Deb crying when she read it, although I knew that given our fragile emotional state, her tears were certainly no indication of this little poem's literary merits. I could have written "Merry Christmas, sweetheart" and she would have wept. Writing it down did help me create a three-dimensional picture in my imagination of this little girl as she lived out her days in the orphanage, receiving kindness and affection where she could find it as she waited for her mommy and daddy to arrive.

As our departure date approached, I started worrying about leaving Gabby at home alone in the dead of winter. She was seventeen and absolutely capable of running the household alone. In fact, she is more capable than I am most days. But still I found things to worry about, about her keeping the fire in the woodstove going and keeping the driveway cleared when it snowed. Gabby told me every day that I didn't need to worry, yet I arranged for the driveway to be plowed and asked Jen Beckley to stop in to make sure she was safe. I also arranged for my parents to drive up from Saint John and stay with Gabby on the weekends so she would not be alone the whole time we were gone.

We packed two large suitcases and a small one. One set of luggage for us, one for Cen Xiao Ru. Her suitcase was filled with little pyjamas, undershirts, receiving blankets, diapers, an electric kettle and power adapter for boiling water and baby bottles, plastic baby bottle liners, and a variety of nipples.

Dave Jewett advised us to pack a small drugstore, which we did, including antibiotics in case she became ill after we received her. He suggested we pack everything we needed to last several days without shopping. We didn't need to be wandering through Chinese department stores trying to decipher diaper labels. He said he understood that it made no sense to be packing so many supplies that had been made in China in the first place, but that we should just do it.

We also packed books about China, books about baby care, some plastic toys, and a handmade doll we received as a gift from my mother's younger sister, Alice. Deb and I were both reading Chinese history in the evenings and tending to the last-minute details, such as getting our immunizations up-to-date, during the day. We also settled on a Canadian name for our daughter. She would be called Lucy. Her full handle would be heavy but we thought quite lovely: Lucy Cen Xiao Ru Nobes Lee.

7

At five o'clock on a freezing cold January morning, a taxi pulled into our driveway. We loaded our three heavy suitcases into the trunk. We had barely slept the night before. We boarded the plane for our trek from Fredericton to Toronto to Vancouver.

The agency sends parents to China in groups. Our group would consist of twelve couples from a variety of Canadian provinces. Another group of twelve couples would travel to another province in China. Our group would travel together, with every minute of the trip arranged and organized by Children's Bridge. On the Toronto flight, we talked with the couple in the seats in front of us, Sue and Ken Worsley, who we discovered were members of our adoption group from Kitchener-Waterloo, Ontario. In Vancouver, we met more members, and while waiting for our flight, we exchanged referral photographs and stories and got to know the people who would share with us this transformative two and a half weeks.

After a gruelling twelve-hour flight, we landed in China, boarded a bus, and drove through the night to our hotel in the marvel that is Shanghai. We travelled across freeways that ran over the top of old neighbourhoods with narrow winding streets and squat stone houses, past an endless parade of high-rises adorned with brightly lit advertisements. Paul Goldberger, writing in the *New Yorker*, observed that Shanghai combines the soul of Houston with the body of Las Vegas: "The sky line of China's largest city has become a strangely exuberant version of the 'Blade Runner' aesthetic, with simple geometries and sharp lines cutting into the sky; it may not be beautiful but, in its staggering scale and intensity, it certainly is awe-inspiring."

We checked into our room in a luxury hotel called the Rendez-vous, an Australian-owned conference facility in downtown Shanghai. We were exhausted. We ordered room service and then tried to sleep off the trip. We had three days to get settled and recover from the jet lag before we travelled to Jiangxi Province. The next morning, we went on a tour of the city's shiny new financial district, a collection of high-rises called the Pudong, built on an island in the Huangpu River, which is a tributary of the Yangtze.

Then we took a boat tour and watched high-rises going up on all sides, while on the water we saw scenes from another time. Old barge riverboats served both as working transports and homes, with construction materials piled high on one side and baby clothes hanging out to dry on the other.

The second day, Deb and I woke early, still trying to adjust to the twelve-hour time difference. We lounged in bed and watched the official China TV news in English. We spent the day in and about the hotel, meeting more members of the group as they arrived in Shanghai from Canada. That night we went out into the city for shopping and dinner with our new friends, Ken and Sue Worsley. We visited a strange, mazelike underground shopping complex, where we bought water and beer, and found a small restaurant where we ate excellent chicken curry and rice. I became very tired at the restaurant and could hardly keep my eyes open through dinner. Deb guided me back to the hotel, where I crashed hard. Deb went down to the hotel's business centre to send an email to Gabby, the beginning of an exchange in which Gabby would send regular and reassuring updates from the home front. She told us Jen had dropped by with a basket of food, including an emergency can of SPAM for when the going got tough.

By morning, I was over my jet lag. The construction noise outside was constant in a city filled with migrant workers who were making a small life in this grand urban landscape. "People carve out spaces in the world to live," I wrote in my journal. "We have such large spaces in Canada. We sometimes make the mistake of believing the spaces will fulfill us, will give us the room to be happy. Deb pointed out a father and son on a busy street today. They had set up a makeshift table where they were sharing a meal. What counts more than spaces are the connections we make with one another. I think we need to remember all this, not just the sights and sounds, the souvenirs, but what we can learn about better ways of living. What we need is to draw ourselves together, not to allow ourselves to fall away in our landscapes, believing there is fulfillment in that."

While we toured Shanghai, we took photographs of young girls. We were thinking all the time about our daughter, and at a certain point, we were only seeing little Chinese girls. She was almost a year old. What did she look like now? What would she look like when she was a toddler, or on her first day of school? On the edge of the river, a crowd of children had gathered around an old man who was flying a giant kite up into the haze that always hangs over the city. That afternoon, we visited a silk factory and bought our daughter red and pink silk pyjamas.

Along with Ken and Sue, we continued to explore the city and then went to eat another good meal the night before we all became new parents. Early in the evening, we happened upon a restaurant called the Always Bar and Grill and decided maybe some western food wouldn't hurt us. We ate and drank with our new friends, surrounded by more western faces in one place than we would see at any point on the trip. The night had an apocalyptic feel. A temperature inversion was driving the smog down onto us. We could see the particulate hanging in the air beneath the street light and taste the soot in our mouths. The air was as thick with smog as the harbour fog I grew up with on the Bay of Fundy shore.

On our last day in Shanghai, we woke up early, had breakfast, packed, and sent last-minute emails at the business office, then delivered our luggage to the lobby and boarded our bus for a tour of the marvellous Shanghai museum, which was another reminder of just how much we didn't know or understand about China. We toured the bronze exhibit, with bells and bronze vessels that were several thousand years old. We also toured the landscape painting galleries. These landscapes are not the magic realism or impressionism of western landscapes but landscapes of the mind. The paintings are generally of mountains and rivers and lakes, often shrouded in mist and clouds, but not of the sort we find in nature. The humans are always tiny in these vast, imaginary natural scenes. Chinese artists spend decades copying the work of the masters before they step outside the lines and begin to improvise and draw on their own imaginative visions. We toured the museum, trying to retain as much information as we could, but also anxious to go find our little one who had been born in the mountains of our imaginations in Jiangxi Province. From the museum we left for the airport.

8

That afternoon, we flew into Nanchang, a city of four and a half million people in the south-central province of Jiangxi, which has a population of forty-four million. The city is built around the Gan River, a tributary of the lower reaches of the Yangtze River. The city of Nanchang is famous within China because the uprising there in August 1927 was the first major engagement of the Chinese Civil War. When Mao Zedong emerged as the leader of communist

China, August 1, 1927, was declared the date of the creation of the People's Liberation Army.

At the Nanchang airport, we loaded our luggage onto the back of a farm truck. We boarded a battered bus, and as we drove through a strange landscape intermingled with farms and high-rise construction, our guide, a woman named Jun Li, who told us to call her Julie, stood up to prepare us for what we were about to experience. Julie had joined our group in Shanghai and would shepherd us through the rest of our trip until we boarded our plane back to Canada. This slim, middle-aged woman with short dark hair and a soft, easy smile took control, standing at the front of the bus with a microphone in one hand and holding on for dear life with the other as the bus lurched down the bumpy road. Julie told us that the children we were about to meet were born of our hearts, not of our bodies. Borrowing the words of Confucius, she told us this was the first step in a journey of a thousand miles. We were to arrive at the Gloria Plaza Hotel and check in. Then at four o'clock, we would gather in a hotel meeting room on the third floor and receive our babies.

Despite all our research, we weren't prepared for the crushing poverty we saw on the drive from the airport. We drove through rice fields and pastures populated by half-starved cattle. The farm families were living in what appeared to be bombed-out concrete houses. We saw children playing in the dirt in yards surrounded by crumbling stone walls. Then we would pass partly constructed new apartment complexes and a car factory. Old landscapes and grinding poverty were juxtaposed with the money that was flowing from the capitalist economic system in the new China. Deb started to cry as she looked at the landscape and the children playing outside, wondering if Xiao Ru's birth parents lived in a place like this.

We pulled up to the hotel and entered the lobby, which had a coffee bar on the right and a restaurant and gift shop on the left. Our bags were unloaded and stacked in the lobby, and we were just lining up to register at the front desk when a parade of men and women came through the revolving door carrying babies all dressed in identical pink and yellow fleece jackets and pants and corduroy shoes fastened with Velcro straps. Someone shouted, "The babies are coming, there they are," and then there was confusion all around us. We pulled our digital camera out of Deb's knapsack and snapped a couple of out-of-focus frames. Deb and I started scanning the crowd for the little worried face we had studied for the past six weeks back in Canada. I couldn't find her, but then I saw Deb walking toward a baby in the arms of a young woman near the elevators. She said to me without taking her eyes off the child, "That's her, there she is."

Deb walked over to the young woman and said, "I think that's our baby." The woman replied "Xiao Ru?" We nodded yes. She said to the little girl in English, "This is your mommy and daddy." There she was, looking older and brighter and plumper than the face in the photograph. We had travelled all these miles and suddenly we found ourselves looking into her dark eyes. Xiao Ru was on the verge of tears, and then the elevator doors opened, the young woman stepped inside, the doors closed and they disappeared.

At that moment, Deb stopped worrying. Xiao Ru was in the building. There was nothing to do but follow the schedule we had been given. We checked in and went to our room and waited for a long half-hour, putting together gift bags for the orphanage workers. Shortly before four o'clock, we took the elevator down to the meeting room on the third floor.

When we walked into the room, we found that Xiao Ru had been transferred to the lap of another orphanage worker, a man. We approached him and told him we were Xiao Ru's parents, and he checked the little girl's name tag and then, without ceremony, handed our daughter to Deb. Xiao Ru cried against her shoulder, and then Deb handed her to me and she buried her face in my neck and cried some more. She was hot and sweating in her fleece suit.

It was a wild and confusing scene. There were a dozen babies in the meeting room in various stages of distress, all crying at the same time. We took photographs of Xiao Ru and of our new friends and their daughters, and posed for a photograph with the orphanage director. I started worrying about feeding Xiao Ru, and made inquiries about what she was eating. I was informed that I could buy a small bag of powdered baby formula called Hero. I gave the money to one of the orphanage staff and held the bag in my hand and started asking questions about how to mix the formula and what she was eating and when. My inquiries were answered mainly with shrugs.

Then we were told we could return to our rooms with the babies and then in an hour, one of us would have to come back to the conference room to complete the first round of paperwork. I had to double check. Had we understood the instructions properly? We hadn't signed a single form and now we were going to be allowed to walk out the door? I found Julie in the crowd and asked her. She smiled gently and waved me to the door.

We carried Xiao Ru back to our room, laid her on the bed, and removed her fleece suit, long underwear, and undershirt and took off her diaper. She was round and appeared to be healthy, but her bottom was covered with diaper rash. We decided we needed to wash her before we applied zinc cream to the rash. We filled a small plastic tub that had been provided in the bathroom and dipped her in. She was screaming, her face red and wet with tears. We covered her bottom with zinc, put on a clean diaper, and dressed her in a soft pink sleeper. She needed to eat.

At that moment, it all came flooding back. It was as if I had been preparing for this moment all of my adult life. I boiled water and sterilized a nipple. I spooned some of the formula powder into a bottle and added hot and cold water until the mixture was lukewarm. I tested the temperature one more time on the inside of my arm. Then I picked her up in the crook of my arm and bounced her gently as I put the nipple in her mouth. She started sucking. I paced back and forth across the floor and she drank till she fell asleep, replacing the nipple with the first two fingers of her right hand, which she had obviously been using to comfort herself in her crib at the orphanage. Deb was so relieved and grateful that my memory had returned at the eleventh hour.

A glorious calm settled on Deb in these first moments, and in many ways, it has stayed with her. She looked so beautiful and happy and filled with strength. When we had Xiao Ru settled in her crib, we started to gather our paperwork and prepare for the process of finalizing the adoption. Up to that point, Deb had handled most of the details. I have never been much good at keeping records and attending to administrative details. I am a big-picture thinker. Deb is a details woman, and I had expected that she was going to carry us through this part of the process. But when we had gathered the bundle of papers, Deb informed me that I was now officially in charge of all paperwork. She was handing off because she wasn't leaving Xiao Ru for a moment. As I took the elevator downstairs with a binder full of papers, I gave myself a good talking to, telling myself that I was an intelligent man and I could do this kind of work. I sat in that conference room and filled out the forms as if I had been pushing paper my whole life.

When I returned to the room, Xiao Ru was awake and lying on the bed beside Deb. I lay down on the other side. For a long time, she shifted her gaze between the two of us, occasionally reaching out to touch our faces and skin with her delicate hands. For weeks, her nannies at the orphanage had been telling her that her mommy and daddy were coming. Now she was looking at a woman with blue eyes of the sort she surely had never seen in her short life and a man with a mop of curly light brown hair. How strange we must have looked to her. But she was sending us powerful signals that she was ready for us. Sometime that night she smiled a cautious smile. She was letting us know that she wanted to be loved and she wanted to love us.

Later that evening, I joined a group of new fathers in the hotel lobby to venture out for supplies at a nearby grocery and drugstore. I needed bottled water for our hotel room. When we stepped outside, I was immediately overwhelmed by the noise on the street. We dodged cars and trucks, motorcycles and bicycles. A man was banging out pots and pans from sheet metal on the sidewalk. We were led up the street by Julie and a local guide named Evelyn, a bright, confident young woman who spoke perfect English and who was making a living and saving for her education by guiding foreign adoption groups. We introduced ourselves in the darkness of the street, and soon we entered a brightly lit, modern supermarket that had a drugstore on the second level.

What a sight we were, this group of frantic new fathers out on a hunting and gathering mission. Evelyn and Julie stood back and watched with amusement as the men in my group started buying everything in sight. They filled their carts with diapers, jars of baby food, bags of powdered formula, nipples, cookies, and juice. I bought bottled water and a few jars of baby food and made my way back to the hotel through the darkness and the cacophony of that wild Sunday night. I dropped the supplies in our hotel room and then left for one more errand. I bought a telephone card, and after I had deciphered the instructions, I dialled two numbers in New Brunswick, where it was early morning. I left a message for Gabby, who I figured had left for school (a good sign, I thought), and then called Walter's number. He picked up the phone. I was glad he was the first one to hear the news. "We got her," I told him. All is well. Spread the word.

I returned to the room to find Deb sleeping in the bed and Xiao Ru sleeping in her crib. About this time, things had settled down enough for me to recognize that our room was filled with a toxic smell of what we suspected was glue applied during the installation of a new carpet. I had to open the window so we could breathe. Street noise filled the room. I sat down and wrote a note to Xiao Ru in my journal: "It's noisy and the air is foul, but we are all in our little space here together. I can hear your sucking sounds in the crib. This is good."

When Xiao Ru woke in the early morning hours, I picked her up and prepared another bottle, fed her, and walked the floors with her in my arms. I was suddenly overwhelmed with feelings of love for this little girl. And so in this strange place, with the terrible air and the street noise rising up through the window, I walked back and forth across the floor with our new daughter in my arms and tears streaming down my face, thankful that all of us in the room had been offered a second chance to find love. Eventually, I laid the sleeping baby back in her crib and dozed until morning.

About six-thirty, I showered and went for a quick breakfast in the hotel restaurant, then went back and watched over the baby and prepared for the day while Deb showered and went down in search of food and coffee. Shortly after eight, twelve families with new babies boarded the bus for the Nanchang Civil Affairs department. Julie and Evelyn shepherded us into an old stone office building that had what appeared to be an open landfill for a backyard. We all filed into a waiting room with wooden benches along the walls. The room was filled with exhausted parents and traumatized children. Some members of our group were quietly weeping. It had been a long night for everyone. We were fortunate that little Xiao Ru's stress-coping mechanism was sleep.

The adoption process is a lesson in what love is about. Loving is a deliberate choice. We all had travelled halfway across the world to be handed babies we had never met, and in the hours and days to come, these babies became our daughters, and we their parents, and all of this because we chose to love each other. We chose to love the babies and the babies chose to love us. We were fortunate that

Xiao Ru was so open to being loved right from the beginning. However, some of the children were aggressively rejecting one parent or another, or both, especially the little girls who had been in foster care and were in mourning over the loss of their families. These feelings would change with time. Julie told us that we had all found a human connection thicker and richer than blood ties.

Everything that day happened with remarkable precision, considering we were in the land that invented bureaucracy. Step one: we had to pose for a family photo and have our thumbprints and Xiao Ru's footprint recorded. We had to wake her up so she could stare bleary-eyed at the camera. Step two: we were interviewed by a stern woman who was the chief bureaucrat of the district. She asked if we would care for the baby and we said we would. She wanted to know how we would care for the child if we were both working. We told her about our plans for parental leave and professional childcare once we returned to work. She wanted to know what plans we had for her education. We told her we planned to see that she was well educated. She made some notes and dismissed us. Step three: we were called one by one into unheated offices with money counters seated behind wooden desks so we could pay our adoption fees to the various government departments, amounts that we had carefully counted out into separate envelopes before we left home. At one point, Ken frantically called me aside and told me he had left some of his money in the hotel and was short. I pushed some cash into his hand and he rushed into one of the rooms to settle his account.

After about two hours, we boarded the bus and drove across town to an even colder office building. We gathered in another waiting room, then lined up in a hallway to be interviewed by another stern woman. When it was our turn, we sat down with her in the office with Julie as our interpreter. Apparently, we passed the test, because we all signed a document that stated we had formally been declared Xiao Ru's parents and she our daughter. Somehow the photograph taken in the building across town had been transferred to this office and glued to the adoption certificate, all of which had been placed in a small red binder. Deb was crying as we walked back down the hall. Ken Worsley, who was waiting for his turn to go into this same office, stopped Deb and asked, "Good tears, bad tears?" They were all good tears, we assured him. Xaio Ru slept through all of this. We returned to the hotel as a legal family.

I napped for about forty-five minutes, the first solid sleep I had had since we left Shanghai, and then went on another water run with Ken. We needed the water to mix formula and sterilize and wash nipples. Hauling water back to our room became my endless mission. Xiao Ru slept most of the day. That afternoon, we had her diaper rash looked at by a doctor, who gave us some ointment, and we moved out of the noxious room into a room on an upper floor that had clean air and a soft, king-sized bed, which made me believe I could survive in this city until the end of the week.

Xiao Ru was quiet during the first couple of days in Nanchang. She only cried when she was put in the tub. One afternoon when I pulled her out of the tub, she started to wail and Deb moved to comfort her. I asked Deb to wait. I wanted Xiao Ru to let some of the grief, tension, and stress go. After a few minutes of good crying, she started to wake up, to contend with us a bit, to smile a little more broadly. Many in our group were desperately trying to stop their daughters from crying. I told them as gently as I could that I think crying is good sometimes. It's how these babies can express themselves, a release. These were the words of a wily veteran. I was falling into my role.

When we went down to dinner that evening at the hotel buffet, an extravagant affair of traditional Chinese food, I brought some rice cereal. I figured it was time to try to get some solid food into our daughter. She looked ready to me. I mixed some of the cereal with formula and offered it to her on a small plastic spoon. She opened her mouth wide and finished the bowl. I don't know if she had been eating solid food before this, but there was no question that she was ready. About eight-thirty, she went to sleep in her crib, and so did we in our lovely new king-sized bed.

In the days that followed, Xiao Ru continued to assert herself. We started hearing more of her voice. She became more and more attached to Deb and would cry whenever her mom left the room. She was still easy to console (except when she was in the tub) and was taking long naps in the morning and afternoon. She continued to sleep through the night and was starting to eat various kinds of solid foods, especially bowls of steamed egg, which we discovered was served in every restaurant in town.

One afternoon we visited the Tang Weng Pavilion, a tourist site just a five-minute walk from the hotel. Inside, we watched a short performance of traditional Chinese music. When the band, two stringed instruments, a flute, and hand bells, started playing the "Happy Song," Xiao Ru started to sing. We figured she must have heard this song in the orphanage. We watched in amazement, happy that she had been exposed to music during her first year and sad that she would be losing this memory when we returned to Canada. "I know you have suffered loss," I wrote in my journal that evening. "I also know you are feeling, craving the love we are offering you. We feel the love coming back."

The night before we left Nanchang, a group of us went to dinner with Evelyn at the Oriental Palace, which is a huge four-storey restaurant near the pavilion. We toured the kitchen area on our way in and saw live birds in cages and fish swimming in tanks, all of which were on the menu. We gathered in a private dinner suite with couches and a big-screen TV. During dinner, a young waitress scooped up Xiao Ru and played with her for most of the meal, making faces at her and swinging her in her arms, all the while speaking to her in Mandarin. Xiao Ru loved every minute of it. When the waitress spoke in Mandarin, we saw the light of understanding go on in our daughter's eyes. "We will get past this language barrier," I wrote that night in my journal. "But it is there. It's a beautiful song you have in your head that you will leave behind when you come with us to Canada."

On the morning we left Nanchang, it rained and the road surface was rough, with construction crews working building new overpasses and off-ramps all the way to the airport. As Deb and I sat in our bus seats with a sleeping Xiao Ru on our laps, we wrapped our arms around each other and cried, for Xiao Ru, for what she had lost somewhere in Jiangxi Province. Her birth family was back there somewhere, down some roadway, this same rain falling on them. What a loss her parents had endured. What profound loss this little girl had endured already in short life. And now we were taking her away from her place and her people. We knew we would need to return to this place with our daughter when she was old enough to remember, to show her where she comes from, as much as we are able to discover. I wrote to Xiao Ru in my journal: "The place you came from is a cold trail. This country is so crowded with people that some little ones get lost. Some also are found."

We wept for Xiao Ru when we were leaving Nanchang, and we also wept for what we had left behind. In the moment we were handed this gift of a little girl, our lives changed irrevocably. We had lost the free and easy intimacy we had found in the past year, our long conversations over dinner and wine, our lazy Saturday mornings in bed. As we watched Xiao Ru sleeping on our laps, there was no question in our minds that we had received a miraculous gift in Nanchang. We were having no feelings of regret, but we left part of ourselves in that hotel. A year later, after we met a couple who had recently visited the Gloria Plaza in Nanchang, Deb told me she almost asked them whether they had seen our ghosts in the hallways.

9

We landed in Beijing after a hard two-hour flight on a crowded plane filled with screaming babies. It was a rough evening, during which we had to try to settle a crying Xiao Ru long enough to get her visa photograph taken. Deb had come down with a cold. The next morning, we went to the international medical clinic for a checkup to satisfy our immigration requirements. When we left the clinic, we told Julie that we would walk back to the hotel. It was refreshing to be out in the crisp morning air with a hint of blue sky. We found a Starbucks down the road from our hotel, and for the first time since we left home, we were drinking decent coffee. During the next week in Beijing, we sat in that shop for hours at a time, with Xiao Ru in a big armchair playing with toys, while we talked with our friends and listened to an endless loop of Rolling Stones songs.

On our final evening in China, all the families went to a restaurant that specializes in Peking duck, roasted in huge, wood-fired ovens. We were tired and sick and the restaurant was smoky, hot, and crowded. The babies, including Xiao Ru, became cranky. After dinner, someone in the group suggested we organize a group photograph of all the babies. I wasn't crazy about the idea, but I put Xiao Ru in a line of babies sitting on the floor along a wall. I wasn't taking pictures, but I was watching my baby, and when she started crying, I said, enough is enough, and walked over and picked her up, and then watched in horror as the whole row of babies toppled sideways like dominos. It was time to go home.

Our leaving day was also the first shared birthday for Xiao Ru and me. We celebrated at Starbucks. As we drove away from the hotel, Julie sang lullabies to the babies. We hugged Julie at the airport and said goodbye. For the first time in three weeks, we were on our own. We boarded the Air Canada flight from Beijing to Vancouver, along with twenty-four other families that had new adopted daughters. The babies were all in various states of trauma. Most of them had diarrhea, and many of their parents were also sick with stomach ailments and colds. We had bought an extra seat on this flight and had three seats across in the centre aisle. We settled Xiao Ru on the seat between us. Many of the families had booked only two seats and some were trying to settle their babies to sleep on their tray tables. Ken and Sue had the three seats in the row in front of us, and Ken joked that we could have auctioned off one of these seats and paid for our entire trip.

Xiao Ru was a tough little travelling baby. She slept most of the way and was in better shape than we were when we landed in Vancouver. When we arrived at the Canada Customs desk, the young man at the desk scanned our papers, looked up with a broad smile, and said, "First, I have to say, congratulations." We moved into a special line, and within minutes, Xiao Ru was declared a permanent resident of Canada. Then we picked up our bags and said hurried goodbyes to our friends. Most of the group just quietly dispersed. Sue Worsley wept as we hugged. Ken finally looked as if he was nearing the end of his endless reserves of strength and good humour.

We spent the night in Vancouver and then had one more day of flying, back to Fredericton. I had been saving one clean shirt for the last day of the trip. As soon as we arrived at the airport, Xiao Ru vomited her breakfast on my shirt. I flew home wearing an "I Love British Columbia" T-shirt.

When we arrived in Fredericton that evening, we were greeted by a crowd of family and friends with balloons and welcome home signs. Some of the "cousins" were there, along with a beaming Dave Jewett and Diane Nadeau. Xiao Ru's grandparents were there. Walter was the first to pick up Xiao Ru and hold her, and then the grandparents had a turn. Gabby, who had been waiting patiently on the sidelines, finally picked up her little sister, and I have a lovely photograph of the big sister biting her lower lip and holding back the tears as she examines Xiao Ru's face. Gabby asked Deb, "Did you know you were getting the most beautiful baby in China?" She carried her new sister to the car and held her hand in the back seat all the way home.

10

Two days after we returned home, I was back in the classroom teaching and Deb began her parental leave with Lucy Xiao Ru. The real work of creating a new family unit began. For the first few weeks, Lucy seemed disoriented by the lack of people. Our walks down lonely country roads in the winter seemed to frighten her. We took her to university hockey games and to the farmer's market and found she was more comfortable in the crowds.

After a month, she became more settled and Deb fell into a routine of mothering a small child. Deb talked to her constantly, and soon our daughter was speaking words in English and making the most of her limited vocabulary. When she learned the word *more*, she attached it to a variety of other words. Our closest friends, Jen Beckley and her husband, Tom, became More Mommy and More Daddy. Their son Sam became Boy Ow, because at twelve, he was growing fast and seemed to be always bumping into things, always wearing a bandage.

My mother was Daddy's Mommy and my father Daddy's Daddy. And so on. Aaron arrived in June. Lucy thought he was the very best thing she had ever seen and promptly named him Boppy, which we decided was a combination of the words *brother* and *happy*. Gabby became Ba, and she called Danielle, who had a baby kitten at her apartment, Baby's Mommy.

Deb's leave ran through the summer, and because I wasn't teaching, we spent as much time as we could at the old house. One weekend, we were joined by the Beckleys. In the morning, when Tom and I found the sea dead calm, we took our double kayak out for a paddle along the shore. As we pushed out on the water, The Brothers looked so close and inviting, I turned the rudder to the right and we paddled out and landed on the front side of the Philip island. We beached the kayak, climbed out, and admired the view of the old house standing straight and true on the point and the waves washing in on the beach in the cove. As I stood on the island, I marvelled at just how far I had come since that summer afternoon seven years earlier when I had returned to the old house and looked out at this island from the shore and watched the rising tide. Tom and I climbed back into the kayak and paddled slowly back to the shore, riding the waves of the incoming tide.

11

Deb reluctantly returned to work in October, and I began a three-month leave from the university to become a full-time homemaker and dad for the first time. We went to the library in the mornings, or to neighbourhood playgroups held at the community hall. I would bring muffins and coffee and socialize with the other moms and dads. I had imagined that I would continue to work in my spare time when I was on leave, but almost immediately my world shrunk and turned on the details of the day. My main goal in the mornings was to keep Lucy busy with play, and then keep her awake in the car on the way home for lunch. A five-minute nap in the car would mean no nap in the afternoon. When I succeeded in keeping her awake, by singing and rubbing her feet or whatever it took, she would sleep in her crib after lunch. Then we took a long walk before supper when Gabby and Deb would return home. While she slept, I played guitar and started writing songs. One of the songs was inspired by a particularly difficult early morning when the two of us spent several hours just staring at each other, with Lucy "finding me wanting" just as Gabby had so many years before:

The sun won't shine
On this cold October morn
The sun won't shine
We've been up since the break of dawn
The sun won't shine
On this cold October morn
Sun won't shine
Till it sees you smile

The rivers won't flow
They won't roll down to the sea
The rivers won't flow
They won't carry you back to me
The rivers won't flow
They won't roll down to the sea
The rivers won't flow
Till they see you smile

I think I see you smiling
Can I hold your hand
I think I see you smiling
Should I strike up the band?

When I returned to work after Christmas, Lucy started attending a daycare in the neighbourhood, and as we drove to our jobs in the city in two cars and rushed back on the highway to pick up Lucy at the end of the day, we decided that we needed to simplify our lives. It seemed everything about our life as a family had changed with the addition of Lucy, and Deb and I were not finding enough time to maintain our own relationship. By the time we had commuted home and picked up Lucy, cooked dinner, brought some order to the house, and got her down to sleep, neither of us had any energy left for the other. We weren't able to do the things that had held us together before our trip to China. We weren't skiing on the weekends, or planning Sunday dinners with our friends. We talked about how much we missed our quiet Saturday mornings together, how we were concerned that we were moving into a new version of the worrisome years. We decided that we needed to change something in our life so that we could make the time we needed for our daughter and for each other.

The following spring, we bought an old two-and-a-half-storey house in downtown Fredericton, a block from the river and a short walk from the university campus and a five-minute drive up the hill to Deb's workplace. It reminded us of the old house by the sea the first time we walked up the narrow staircase and down the hall and saw the window that looked out toward the river. I immediately fell in love with downtown living. On Saturday mornings, we walked to the farmer's market. We sold one of our cars and gave away or sold many of the possessions we had but didn't need, especially in a house that had small closets and no storage space. I discovered that on a smaller lot my world felt larger than it had before, that the streets and sidewalks and parks were now ours. Gabby, who had moved to an apartment in the city and was working and saving money to attend university in the fall, moved back in with us for the summer. Here, once again, we began to create a new family home.

12

On the morning of our third wedding anniversary, I gave Deb a card with her coffee and told her how much I love her and how I count myself among the most fortunate of men. It was one of the days when I was writing in my home office, and on those days, Deb would drop Lucy off at preschool on her way to work. I helped her during the launch of the day. I read books to Lucy while she ate breakfast and then got her dressed while Deb showered and got ready for work. I packed Lucy's bag, stuffed her into her snowsuit, and loaded her into the car.

After they drove away on this particular morning, I picked up the phone and called my favourite florist, the same one who had designed Deb's wedding bouquet. I ordered a small arrangement of cut flowers and asked that they be delivered to her office before noon. The entire transaction took about five minutes and cost me about twenty-five bucks. After I made that call, I turned on my computer and settled in for a day of work.

When Deb arrived home that evening, she told me how much she appreciated the flowers and that many of the women at her office were envious because their husbands never send them flowers. For a moment, I basked in the glory of being a rising star in the order of husbands, but later that evening, I started wondering how this could be. How many of us are taking for granted the people we love most, and in the process, missing out on the possibilities of real love in our lives?

I would never presume that I have reached the point where I have arrived and can simply sit back and watch the world unfold before me. I'm reminded of my slips and shortcomings as I stumble through my days and weeks of work, of mopping up and making love. I think every day about how fragile and tenuous all of this is, and how fortunate I am to have found what I've found for as long as we've been able to keep it. If I were to die tomorrow, I would have wished for more time, but never regretted for a moment the generous chances for love and friendship I have been given.

However, for all of us twice-married men there is a small cautionary note fixed in the back of our minds — and if the cautionary note isn't there, it should be. Even though I was trying to do better the second time around, even though I found a greater love than I ever thought was possible, I can't forget the frightening odds that more than half of all twice-married men will end up twice-divorced. A friend told me once that in any marriage "there is always a good reason to get divorced." He's right. And we will either find ways to hold on to our love, or we'll have reached the end of the line. The challenge is finding ways to adapt to change.

In his book *The Age of Unreason,* published in 1989, business management guru Charles Handy explores how technological change is transforming the working world. Handy makes a case for a new way of thinking about the way we work. He suggests that to reinvent work we need a new term — portfolio work — to describe the different kinds of work we do that fit together to form a whole. For example, I spend part of my life teaching, part of my life writing, part of it organizing and running my department, and reading, and working at home. He argues that this kind of portfolio thinking should be applied to modern marriages.

"Everyone will live a portfolio life for part of their lives," Handy writes. "Most people will match that with a portfolio marriage. A portfolio marriage is not a recipe for polygamy, a different partner for each day or night, nor is it an invitation to serial monogamy, a sequence of husbands or wives. Rather it is a way of adjusting a marriage to the differing demands of a changing portfolio in life." Marriages need to be constantly renegotiated. We need to be flexible, Handy writes, or we'll break. "Too often, serial monogamy or a change in partner is the way many people match their need for a marriage with their need for change."

In the mid-1970s, Handy and a researcher from the London Business School studied a group of twenty-three business managers and their spouses to try to find out what kinds of marriages they had. All the participants considered themselves happily married. They did some personality profile testing, which placed the participants in the study into four general categories. He named the high achievers who had little time or interest in helping at home, Thrusters; the high achievers who were also interested in caring and helping, Involved; the people whose only distinguishing characteristic was that they were autonomous, Loners; and those who were most interested in caring for others and weren't interested in achievement and advancement, Carers.

More than half the women studied but none of the men were found to be Carers. Only one of the women was a Thruster. Handy notes that the distribution along gender lines would certainly be very different even a decade later when he wrote about it in his book; however, he thinks his observations about the twenty-three marriages are still sound. The most common pattern was a Thrusting man married to a Caring woman. The second most common pattern was a marriage of two Involved people. There were also two marriages of Loners, and two marriages of Thrusters.

The Thruster and Carer marriage is the classic partnership from the mid-twentieth-century nuclear family. "It was the husband's job to earn the living, the wife's to run the home and look after the children," Handy writes. "He looked after the drink in the house, she the food, he tended the vegetables, she the flowers. He had his friends, she hers. There were no overlapping friends except for family." Conversations in these households tended to sound like event planning instead of exchanges of ideas. To relieve stress, they participated in activities separate from each other.

The marriages of the two Involved people were different. They came from similar backgrounds and had lives that were intertwined in every respect. "All friends were joint friends, all activities joint activities. Mealtime conversations were about ideas, were full of argument and discussion. When they had stress problems they shared them, drinking copious cups of coffee or cheap red wine late into the night, then going off to be concerned but achieving workers the next day. Life was intense, interesting, and, yes, involved."

The marriages of the two Thrusters were competitive partnerships, with two full-on careers, no children, and lots of mutual affection. These were the original dinkies (dual income no kids yet). Handy noted that it was easy for the two Thrusters to slip into the realm of the Loners, where two people would be together but alone. "They lived their own lives, timing things precisely in the case of one couple, so that he would arrive home just in time for her to leave to go out to her work with one of them at home with the children. They were content, they said, and happy — two trees together in the wood, together but not touching, or even talking very much."

Handy wasn't trying to chart a course for the ideal marriage. He noted that many of these marriages would have changed over time. Most started out as two Involved people, and then when children came, these marriages often transformed into a Thruster (man) and Carer (woman) pattern. And then when a woman went back into the workforce, they became a Thruster and Thruster pattern.

He concluded that there is no right or wrong pattern for a marriage. What is clear is that that we need to be open to change, and to changing patterns in our lives. "People clearly *can* change their pattern if both parties want to. Separation and divorce often seem to occur because one partner wants to change the pattern and the other does not." When we have rapidly changing portfolio lives, we need flexible portfolio marriages. "If they do not realize that it is only the *patterns* which are changing, then it is the *relationship* which breaks. Portfolio thinking *and* talking are both essential."

These kinds of negotiations are the most difficult moments in a marriage. Deb and I are working at this. As a news producer, she is generally busier than I am, at least in the sense that her day is more inflexible. I go through periods at the university when I am flooded with work, and then there are long stretches when I am writing and I have the time to carry the load at home. Then when my writing flounders, I start complaining about not having enough creative space to work, and we try to find ways to trade off housework and child care. I have Thruster tendencies, although they have diminished somewhat since I left the daily news business. Deb has these same tendencies in her work for a nightly television news show, so finding a way forward when we are both consumed with work can strain our partnership.

When we reach the point where renegotiation is necessary, we tend to struggle and argue and both demand more support from the other — then we sit down and quietly begin a negotiation that usually involves each of us making some compromises in our work life and expectations at home to try to find a balance that works for both of us. The balance works until circumstances change at home or at work, and then the negotiations begin again. Our partnership has evolved from when we were both parenting teenagers, to the brief period when the teens had left us or grown up and needed little parenting, to the marriage we have now as parents of a young daughter. Nothing about these transitions was easy, but this is the work of love that carries with it the greatest of rewards in this life.

On the evening of my third anniversary as a twice-married man, as I contemplated the flowers and the reaction to them in Deb's office, I thought that perhaps there is something to be learned from my experience on the road of second chances. On that day, I began to write some things down, and over time this story emerged from my writing room, a story about darkness and light, second chances, and learning what it means to love another.

13

Lucy turned three the January after we moved to the city. In the spring, we made plans to travel to the Greek islands. It was nine years since Deb and I had fallen in love and I had turned my home and family upside down. I had been nine years on the perilous road of second chances. They had been the hardest and the best years of my life.

I had travelled to Greece two decades earlier after completing my undergraduate degree, and I had always planned to return. But I never had found the time. My first trip to Greece was part of a

European tour with my former roommate and long-time friend Pete Dale. We planned the trip for months over beers in Halifax barrooms, purchased plane tickets and rail passes, and then in the weeks before our departure date, I fell ill with mononucleosis, that college disease born of late nights and general bad living. When our departure date arrived, I was lying in bed at my parents' home in New Brunswick with a high fever and strict doctor's orders not to travel. I reluctantly invoked my travel insurance. Pete had no choice but to begin the trip alone, and we promised to meet up somewhere once I had recovered enough to travel.

Late one night a couple weeks later, my mother answered a telephone call in the middle of the night. Over a crackling line, she had a broken conversation with Pete, during which he told her he was on the Greek island of Crete. Before the line failed completely, my mother managed to write down the word Loutros and some dates. He would wait there for me to arrive.

The next morning, my mother and I got out the map and found the tiny village on the south coast of the island. I was still sick, running a low-grade fever most days, but I decided it was now or never, so I told my worried parents that I was well enough to travel, and I set out to find Pete.

I landed in Athens, and the next morning, I flew on a small plane to Crete. From the airport I took a bus over the top of the island to the south coast to a town where the roads end and the more distant villages like Loutros can be reached only by boat. I hired a water taxi, which followed the coastline until we reached a cove and a beach and a scattering of houses. I stepped off on the dock with no idea whether Pete would arrive that day or several days later, although I had absolute confidence that he would come. I found a small taverna on the beachfront, where I ordered beer and fresh fish and settled in with a book for what I figured might be a long wait. About an hour later, I heard Pete say my name. I looked up and saw him standing in front of my table, tanned and scruffy from his weeks of travelling, his long, dark hair stuffed under a broad-brimmed straw hat. We drank together until the bar closed and caught up on the events of the past weeks.

In the morning, we left Loutros on the water taxi. We toured around Crete for a couple of days before boarding a ferry to the island of Santorini. We had no schedule for the trip other than to spend a couple of weeks in Greece. We stayed a month. We found a room in a town on Santorini's coast and sunned ourselves on the island's black sand beaches. From there we travelled to Ios, an island of fine beaches, with all-night bars and discos built into an old Greek town on a hillside.

After two weeks on Ios, I decided I needed to get away on my own to experience the Greek world I had been reading about in my studies, so I made arrangements to meet Pete in a week in the port city of Piraeus and took a ferry to the mainland. I spent a day in Athens touring the acropolis and the museums and said a prayer before the temple of Athena, the goddess who had watched over Odysseus and championed his homecoming. Then I took a bus north to Delphi to visit the site of the oracle. I stood on the brink of a long, misty gorge that extends miles south to the sea and understood for the first time why the Greeks considered this magical place the centre of the world. I travelled south along the Peloponnesus to visit the ruins of Mycenae, the home of Agamemnon, the leader of the Greek army at Troy. I toured the magnificent theatre and temple ruins at Epidaurus. By the end of that week, I had connected place to the poetry I loved.

I met Pete at the port in Piraeus, and after a night in Athens, we boarded a ferry to Italy and continued north from there, visiting France, Switzerland, Germany, Denmark. Six weeks later, after a drug-crazed week in Amsterdam, I flew home to begin my graduate degree at Dalhousie University. Two years after I returned from that trip, I was married, and my dream of returning to Greece was put on hold for more than two decades — which is too long to put any dream on hold.

I wanted to return to the Greek islands, in particular. During my time there, I had seen beautiful beachfront hotels, and I always held in the back of my mind that some day when I had some money I would return, possibly with my family, to stay in one of those places.

Deb and I chose the island of Naxos, the largest island in the Cyclades, as our destination. We flew from Fredericton to Montreal to Munich to Athens. When we arrived at the Athens airport, Lucy was asleep in her fuzzy pink pyjamas. We were all tired and dirty, feeling ill from a lack of sleep and eating airline food. We laid Lucy down to sleep on a bench and sipped bottled water while we waited to board our final flight to the island. When Lucy woke up, she asked where she was. We told her we were in Greece. She looked around at the crowds in the airport, then outside at the planes and cars and asphalt. Finally, she asked, "Where's the beach?"

We took one more short flight, and after a hair-raising taxi ride down the island's narrow twisting roads, we checked into our hotel in a beach community called Agia Anna. We ate a meal in the seaside taverna called the Palatia, which was connected to our hotel. That evening, while Deb slept, I took Lucy for a walk in her stroller to help her fall asleep. We walked down a narrow alley, the soft air filled with the sounds of the waves and the scent of honeysuckle.

We had chosen Naxos because it has a permanent population that still lives a traditional Greek life and has not given itself over entirely to the tourism industry. The main town was built above ancient ruins from the Mycenean age, constructed in stages on the rocky hillside above the sea. The town is a maze of alleyways with shops and apartment homes, hidden gardens and terraces, each little space made beautiful in its own way with painted white stucco and flowers and vines. In the mountains, the most distant town of

Apeiranthos allows no cars inside the town proper, and the homes are connected by narrow pedestrian streets paved with marble stones that open into ancient agora under shade trees hundreds of years old.

In the mornings, I bought fresh bread and cheese at a market a stone's throw from our apartment. We spent our days relaxing on the beach, sightseeing, and making trips into the town to explore and shop. In the afternoons on the beach, we ordered cold beer and exquisite tomato balls, a sweet concoction of tomatoes, garlic, and dill, fried in island-pressed olive oil. We ate out in restaurants or bought groceries and cooked simple meals of stir-fried fresh tomatoes, eggplant, potatoes, and garlic, all bursting with flavour that is missing from the produce we buy during the long Canadian winters.

Life on this Greek island is played out in public spaces, where friendships are formed through conversation and shared meals. There is a pace to life on the islands that is entirely foreign to the North American way of living. Shops and businesses open in the morning and then shut down in the afternoons for a meal and siesta. The shops reopen about seven and then about nine, the tavernas start to fill up with families, who gather in groups to eat. They stay up talking and eating and drinking till well past midnight.

The men gather in groups around tables in tavernas, as they have for hundreds of years, swinging a string of Komboloi beads in their hands, a stress-relieving ritual. They converse with one another in the animated fashion that reminded me that Greek is meant to be spoken, and that the dialogues of Plato and poetry of Homer and Sophocles lose so much of their meaning in translation and in the quiet, restrained discussions of university classrooms. The old men who gathered on the waterfront seemed to be just watching the day unfold, a glass of ouzo in one hand and swinging Komboloi in the other, caught up in the conversation of the moment, so that nothing at all mattered other than the space they were in right now.

It is this understanding of what it means to be free and to live a good life that the Athenians were fighting for on the plains at Marathon, when a small Greek army broke the Persian line and drove the invading army back into the sea. This is why the great Athenian playwright Aeschylus, who fought as a foot soldier in the hoplite army at Marathon, asked that his epitaph read as follows: "Beneath this stone lies Aeschylus, son of Euphorion, the Athenian, who perished in the wheat-bearing land of Gela; of his noble prowess the grove of Marathon can speak, or the long-haired Persian who knows it well." He wanted to be remembered not for his honours in dramatic competitions in Athens but for his defence of freedom of these most simple of life's pleasures, the freedom to gather, and think and speak as we please.

On this island, I was reminded that while we spend so much of our lives working too hard to make the money we need to accumulate the things we don't need, these simple pleasures are what matter. I suppose I am too tied to my work and my home to do it now, but I could imagine some day giving it all up and replacing it with a small apartment on an island such as this, where I could spend my days in pursuit of these simple pleasures of good food and drink, friends and conversation.

During our two and a half weeks on Naxos, I woke up early every morning, tiptoed out of our apartment, walked through the deserted courtyard to the beach, and set up my computer on a table in a deserted taverna by the ocean to write while Deb and Lucy slept. My favourite writing place was at a table at the Palatia, at the edge of the deck, just off the sand, a stone's throw from the waves. About nine or ten, depending on how the writing was going, I'd check to see if the curtains were open in our apartment, and if they were, I knew my girls were awake and I'd join them for breakfast. Lucy, who we decided is the most adaptable child in the world, ate mountains of Greek food, preferred to play naked on the beach, and when tired asked to go back to our "Greece home" to play quietly in the apartment and sleep. The people of Naxos love children and made a fuss over Lucy everywhere we went, offering her pieces of chocolate and small gifts. One young shopkeeper gave her a necklace of coloured wooden beads that she wore throughout the trip.

On Naxos, we met a couple from Germany whose daughter was adopted from Peru. Lucy and this little girl kept staring at each other, somehow seeing each other in their dark hair and dark eyes, with parents that looked different from them. Their little girl from Peru spoke German. Our little girl from China spoke English. We all went to dinner one evening and celebrated our time on this island with a long, expansive meal, aided by the fact that our new friends spoke Greek and helped us order. The couple told us of their journey to adopt this beautiful and strong little girl, and how when they took her at the age of two from the orphanage in Lima into the mountains, she had seen rain for the first time. After we finished our meal, the waiters continued to bring us complimentary ouzo, and when we finally left the table with our sleeping little girls, we walked back home listening to the waves crash in the darkness.

There is a texture to the light on the Greek islands, which rises from behind the mountains in the mornings to saturate the clear water and reflect and refract between the sea and the whitewashed buildings and soft blues in the sky. The poet Sappho called the emergence of this light "goldsandaled Dawn." As the days passed, we became filled up with this light and with each other.

When I looked at Deb in this light, I was reminded of a scene in the novel *Fugitive Pieces*, which Deb had read to me on the beach in Bathurst years ago — on the trip that saved us. The novel's hero, Jacob Beer, has found love, a second-chance love, and he has returned with her to the Greek island of Idhra, where they are eating at a restaurant that smells of olive oil and fresh thyme and lemons. His love, Michaela, is drinking wine and eating fresh bread and olives. They are joined by a friend, and during the course of the meal, Jacob admires his companions from the other side of the table. "I look at their faces across the table. Our guest's gentle privacy, his restrained affection, and Michaela, bursting with health and radiating pleasure, looking — is it possible? — like a woman well loved."

When I first heard Deb read this passage to me, I wasn't able to say that I was looking at a woman well loved, although I wanted to be the kind of man who could love a woman in this way. As the days passed on Naxos and I admired Deb's beauty in the magic light of the island and looked into her eyes that reflected the blues of the sea and sky, I allowed myself to believe that I was looking at a woman well loved.

14

All of us long for a homecoming. But what about long-suffering Penelope? She waited for twenty years for Odysseus to return to Ithaca from the Trojan War. Why did she wait so long? Penelope expressed her longing in this way:

> *Whatever form and feature I had, what praise I'd won,*
> *the deathless gods destroyed that day the Achaeans*
> *sailed away to Troy, my husband in their ships,*
> *Odysseus — if he could return to tend my life*
> *the renown I had would grow in glory.*

George Dimock tells us that the Greek expression *ton emon bion amphipoleuoi*, normally translated as "tend to my life," is perhaps better rendered as "cultivate my life." The verb *amphipoleuoi* is used in agricultural contexts, about farmers tending to their gardens.

Penelope wants Odysseus to return and cultivate her life. She wants him to be present in her days and fussing about her, as a careful and constant gardener tends to his plants. Surely this is a wonderful expression of the nature of love. In love, we choose to cultivate the life of another, and to have ours cultivated in turn.

When Odysseus returns to his home and slaughters the suitors in a bloodbath in the great hall, he finally encounters Penelope. She thinks he must be her husband, but she tests him to be sure. She tells him that she would like to take him to their bed, but that she may have to bring in a bed because their marriage bed has been removed. He responds in anger, telling her that the bed he constructed before he left could never have been moved.

> *There was a branching olive-tree inside our court,*
> *grown to its full prime, the bole like a column, thickset.*
> *Around it I built my bedroom, finished off the walls*
> *with good tight stonework, roofed it over soundly*
> *and added doors, hung well and snugly wedged.*
> *Then I lopped the leafy crown of the olive,*
> *clean-cutting the stump bare from roots up,*
> *planing it round with a bronze smoothing adze —*
> *I had the skill — I shaped it plumb to the line to make*
> *my bedpost, bored the holes it needed with an auger.*
> *Working from there I built my bed, start to finish,*
> *I gave it ivory inlays, gold and silver fittings,*
> *wove the straps across it, oxhide gleaming red.*
> *There's our secret sign, I tell you, our life story!*

203

This bed is a work of art only possible in the imagination. This description of the great rooted bed is their life story, their secret sign, because this is what marriage is, a union rooted in nature, and a work of the imagination, that in time can become art. This kind of love endures when it is well rooted and when it is cultivated.

Odysseus has come home by choice. He has chosen Penelope and the hardship that accompanied his return. After Penelope tests her husband and he passes, they spend the night making love and talking, and the goddess Athena sees to it that the night is extended to allow them the extra hours they need for their reunification. Homer makes it clear that what they have found with each other makes life possible; it has saved their lives.

> *Joy, warm as the joy that shipwrecked sailors feel*
> *when they catch sight of land — Poseidon has struck*
> *their well-rigged ship on the open sea with gale winds*
> *and crushing walls of waves, and only a few escape, swimming,*
> *struggling out of the frothing surf to reach the shore,*
> *their bodies crusted with salt but buoyed up with joy*
> *as they plant their feet on solid ground again,*
> *spared a deadly fate. So joyous now to her*
> *the sight of her husband, vivid in her gaze,*
> *that her white arms, embracing his neck*
> *would never for a moment let him go . . .*

Odysseus and Penelope have been reunited not because of some kind of natural animal attraction but because of their rational decision to take up each other and build a life together, to cultivate each other's lives. The homecoming is not an ending but a beginning. Surely this invitation to create families of the imagination and the heart is one of the great gifts of marriage in the modern world. If marriage was once rooted in and limited by economic necessity and social class and blood lines, we have been offered a chance to create our own great rooted beds, our own secret signs, and our own life stories.

15

During our final days on Naxos, we experienced an invasion of Greeks from the mainland who came to celebrate the May long weekend, which is the feast of Agiou Pneumatos, the ascension of the Holy Spirit, fifty days after Easter. It is a religious holiday, but it presents the population of Athens the opportunity to visit the Greek islands. By Saturday afternoon, our sleepy island had already taken on the atmosphere of a holiday beach resort as hundreds of Greeks from the mainland poured off the ferries and rushed to the beaches to celebrate the beginning of summer, sunbathing, drinking, and swimming in the sea, which was growing warmer every day. We were suddenly surrounded by fashionably dressed Europeans in giant sunglasses and tiny bathing suits talking on their cell phones, offering us a glimpse of what this island becomes in high season.

We were also treated to the spectacle of a large wedding, which was held on the beach at Agia Anna. Deb spotted them first, gathering the day before at a beach club, the Banana, next door to our hotel taverna. Deb saw a dozen people arrive together and gather in a circle and order drinks. We like to spy and eavesdrop, a journalist's habit, and she sized up the group and the slight tensions in the air, the two sets of parents and greetings and hand shaking, and said that she thought we were about to witness a wedding. I joined in the spying game and picked the bride out of the group. She had long blonde hair, was wearing jeans and long sleeves, and was being careful to stay out of the sun. The manager of our hotel confirmed later in the day that the hotel was indeed filled with a wedding party.

The Banana is a beautifully decorated open-air beach club. It has a much more hip decor than the Palatia, with its square marble-topped tables, woven cane seat chairs, and stone patio. The Banana is all curves and couches, with palm trees growing up through a roof fashioned from bamboo stems. The whitewashed benches inside are decorated with bright green and turquoise flowered cushions, shells hang from strings in the doorway, and a wooden boardwalk extends out onto the sand.

By dawn on the morning of the wedding, the staff had removed the palm-leaf umbrellas and faded yellow lounge chairs from the beach and replaced them with white shade tents and round tables draped with white linens and cutlery wrapped in white napkins. Everything glistened in the afternoon sun.

Shortly before two o'clock, about two hundred people arrived in Agia Anna, took off their shoes, and walked across the sand to a white stucco Greek orthodox chapel, built on a rocky bluff at the end of the beach in honour of Agios Nikolaos, the saint who safeguards travellers on the seas. A shade tarp was raised over the courtyard outside the tiny chapel so that the witnesses could stay cool while they watched the exchange of vows. After the ceremony, the guests walked back to the Banana club, where waiters dressed in white shirts were placing chilled wine, beer, and water at the centre of each table. They laid out an expansive buffet and continued to deliver what appeared to be an endless flow of alcohol to the tables.

After the meal, the dancing began. Musicians with violin and bouzouki played traditional Greek songs, and the guests held hands and danced in circles on the sand. The bride, with her long blonde hair curled and decorated with white ribbons, wore a strapless, layered, off-white lace wedding gown, and she looked happy and gorgeous. She led the dancing with her husband, who was dressed in an open-neck white silk shirt and beige linen pants, also looking happy and beautiful. We watched for a while and then returned to our room to rest before heading out for dinner.

When I walked by late in the afternoon, the wedding party had picked up steam. A DJ was spinning a medley of pop dance songs, and more of the tables had been moved to create a dancing space on the sand. Some of the young male dancers had stripped to the waist, and others were dancing and talking on their cell phones at the same time. The young women had kicked off their high heels and were dancing barefoot at the edge of the waves outside the tents. It was a marvellous coming together of family and friends, young and old dancing together on the boardwalk, a sullen teenage girl in the alley beside the Palatia sneaking a cigarette and talking on her phone. The bride was changing dance partners every few minutes, hugging and kissing the guests and posing for photographs. Young love is a beautiful thing indeed, and love at any age is worth celebrating.

Early in the evening, we went out to dinner at our favourite taverna down the shore with some new German friends we had met on the beach, who had a little blonde-haired girl Lucy's age. The taverna, called O Fotis, was a family affair. Fotis waited tables and acted as the host. His wife cooked in the kitchen, and his daughter and son waited tables. The restaurant had a wood-fired grill and an open patio paved with marble stones. Across the road on a small strip of pavement next to the beach, Fotis had made a two-table patio. He strung lights up in the trees and set out two tables and chairs, another example of how the islanders make the most of small spaces. Fotis walked across the road to serve the patrons who wanted to sit a little closer to the ocean. The family served simple but exquisite meals of grilled meats, freshly sliced tomatoes, and tzatziki sauce with fresh, creamy yogurt laced with so much garlic that it almost burned our mouths. Fotis took a liking to Lucy and gave her chocolates each time we visited. That evening we stayed too late and Lucy became exhausted and started crying. We were having no luck consoling her, so Fotis took her out the back door past the kitchen to meet their pet goose. The goose had been raised by his daughter and had imprinted on her. It followed her everywhere she went. Every afternoon she took the goose swimming in the ocean. Fotis and the goose made Lucy forget her fatigue long enough for us to settle the bill and gather our things for a peaceful departure.

We walked home slowly, watching the moonlight reflecting off the waves. Lucy fell asleep in her stroller. We took one more walk down to see the wedding party. Pop music blared and the dancing continued. A cluster of young people with arms in the air moved on the beach. We returned to our hotel, went up to our room, closed the windows. Deb found our earplugs so we could sleep as the music and party went on into the night.

The next morning, I awoke at dawn, drank a cup of coffee, gathered my computer and notebooks, and walked one last time down to the taverna beside the beach outside our hotel. The party had ended sometime in the night, and the wind had blown strips of paper confetti into the corners of the stone courtyard. The sun was rising over the mountains behind the hotel, but it would be several hours before its light would reach the water. I left my computer and notebooks on my usual table at the edge of the sand in front of the Palatia and walked down the beach along the boardwalk in front of the Banana club. The ground was littered with wine bottles, beer cans, plastic water bottles, and cigarette butts. The white tents and round dinner tables were still on the beach, the metal folding chairs that had been decorated with white cloth were stacked inside the beach club. All around me were the footprints the dancers had left in the sand. Somewhere among them were the footprints of the bride and groom.

I returned to my table and lost myself in writing until the church bells rang, calling the villagers to morning prayers. Deb and Lucy would be rising soon, and it was time for me to make coffee and shop for breakfast supplies, so I shut down my computer, stood up and stretched, crossed the sand to the water, and continued out into the crashing surf where I watched the morning light penetrate the sea. I splashed water on my face and neck and then returned to the beach and dried myself in the morning sun under the blue Mediterranean sky. I gathered my things from the table, picked up my sandals, and walked across the cool stones of the courtyard, filled with gratitude and wonder that we had come to this place, and that we had found our way home.

Acknowledgements

During the writing of this book I received the McCain Award from St. Thomas University that offered me a course release and the space I needed to complete the first draft of the manuscript. For that, I thank my university colleagues and the McCain family of New Brunswick.

In many ways, the writing of this book was a collaborative effort with the people who lived the story. Dr. Kersti Covert and Dorothy Frazier both agreed to be interviewed and then read sections of the manuscript and helped to correct my mistakes. My family's lifelong friend the Reverend Michael LeBlanc offered encouragement and suggestions. Katy Haralampides helped me to understand the science of the Bay of Fundy tides. Jen and Tom Beckley taught me about the nature of true friendship. Barry Craig and Sara MacDonald, my colleagues at St. Thomas University, allowed me to include their story in my narrative and agreed to sit for interviews. They also read the manuscript and offered insights about philosophical and theological questions.

My parents read the manuscript and sent me many valuable corrections, both factual and literary. My sister Susan was a constant support during the process of writing this book and my sister Sadie helped me live through this period of my life in general. My brother Walter generously allowed me to write about a difficult time in our lives and kept his sense of humour throughout.

My children Danielle, Gabrielle, and Aaron all read the manuscript, helped to correct my mistakes in the telling of the story, and have continued to love me all these years.

Susanne Alexander, my long-time publisher, was a partner from the beginning of the project. Julie Scriver, who designed the book, also believed in the project from the beginning and offered her support at critical times. Akoulina Connell helped me stay focussed and encouraged me at deadline times. Heather Sangster combed the manuscript for mistakes and inconsistencies in the best tradition of copy editing.

My brilliant editor Bethany Gibson encouraged me, challenged me, and shaped this book from the beginning and at every stage.

My partner in life, Deb Nobes, lived this story with me, encouraged me to begin writing it down, and then put up with me while I wrestled with the narrative. Her smarts, good love, and sense of story are everywhere in these pages and in the larger story we are living every day.

Acknowledgements

On translations:

Excerpts from Homer's *The Odyssey* are from the masterful translation by Robert Fagels. Copyright © 1996 by Robert Fagels. Reprinted by permission of Penguin Books.

Excerpts from the translation of Sophocles's *Oedipus at Colonus* are also by Robert Fagels. Copyright © 1984 by Robert Fagels. Published by Penguin Books.

Excerpts of the Greek poet Sappho are from the elegant work by poet and classicist Anne Carson. In the magical ways that one word leads to another, I discovered Carson's work on Sappho after we had settled on the title for this book. Her book *If Not, Winter: Fragments of Sappho* copyright © 2002 by Anne Carson was first published by Alfred A. Knopf. Her fine work in general challenged and enriched my understanding of the meaning of *eros*.

Translations of Aristotle's *Nichomachean Ethics* are by Terence Irwin. Copyright © by 1999 by Terence Irwin. Published by Hackett Publishing Company.

The Dark Year

2   Greg Brown's lyrics from the song, "Worrisome Years," are from the album *Down in There* copyright © 1990 on Red House Records. Reprinted by permission.

I am indebted to Allan Bloom's commentary on Leo Tolstoy's *Anna Karenina*. The commentary is part of his larger work *Love and Friendship* copyright © 1993 by Allan Bloom. Published by Simon and Schuster. All references to Bloom are from this book and are reprinted by permission of the Estate of Allan Bloom.

3 Lewis Lapham has used the expression "wilderness of our experience" in his writing and in interviews about journalism. Most recently, he used this expression and the quote about finding truth in stories in his essay, "The Gulf of Time," which appeared in the first edition of *Lapham's Quarterly*, published in October 2007. Available online at http://www.laphamsquarterly. org.

The excerpt from "I'm Just a Regular Asshole" was composed by Michel Thériault. The excerpt is reprinted by permission of Michel Thériault.

The phrase "the great work of love" appears in Elizabeth Barrett Browning's sonnet, "X," from *Sonnets from the Portuguese*, first published in 1850. Reissued in 2004 by Kessinger Publishing.

5 *Charlotte's Web* copyright © 1952 by E.B. White was reissued in 1980 by HarperCollins Publishers.

10 *Marriage, a History: From Obedience to Intimacy, or How Love Conquered Marriage* copyright © 2005 by Stephanie Coontz was published by Viking Penguin. Excerpts reprinted by permission of the publisher.

11 My edition of *Zen and the Art of Motorcycle Maintenance: An Inquiry into Values* by Robert Pirsig was published by Bantam New Age in 1981. The original book was published in the United States by William Morrow in 1974. Excerpts from *Zen and the Art of Motorcycle Maintenance* copyright © 1974 by Robert M. Pirsig are reprinted by permission of The Random House Group Ltd. and HarperCollins Publishers.

13 *News Is a Verb: Journalism at the End of the Twentieth Century* copyright © 1998 by Pete Hamill was published by Ballantine Books.

The excerpt from *The Meaning of Life* copyright © 2007 by Terry Eagleton is reprinted by permission of Oxford University Press.

Eros the Bittersweet copyright © 1986 *by Anne Carson* explores the work of Sappho and the nature of *eros*. It was originally published by Princeton

University Press in 1986 and reissued by Dalkey Archive Press in 2005. Excerpts from *Eros the Bittersweet* are reprinted by permission of Dalkey Archive Press.

An excerpt from *Made for Happiness: Discovering the Meaning of Life with Aristotle* copyright © 2001 by Jean Vanier is reprinted by permission of House of Anansi Press.

18 Todd Snider's song, "Just in Case," was released in 2000 on the album *Happy to Be Here* by Oh Boy records. An excerpt from the lyrics is reprinted by permission of Bro 'N Sis Music, Inc. and Keith Sykes Music.

19 An excerpt from *The Unity of the Odyssey* by George E. Dimock copyright © 1989 by the University of Massachusetts Press is reprinted by permission of the University of Massachusetts Press.

20 Excerpts from *Fugitive Pieces* copyright © 1996 by Anne Michaels are reprinted by permission of McClelland & Stewart Ltd.

The quote from Thomas Burnet is part of the epigraph that appeared with an early version of "The Rime of the Ancient Mariner" by Samuel Taylor Coleridge.

21 The excerpt from *No Great Mischief* copyright © 1999 by Alistair MacLeod is reprinted by permission of McClelland & Stewart Ltd.

The Things Which Are

2 George Dimock's observations about the name of Odysseus appear in *The Unity of the Odyssey* and in various other writings, including his translations of *The Odyssey,* which in turn influenced Robert Fagels's reading of the poem.

7 Excerpts from *The Road Less Traveled: A New Psychology of Love, Traditional Values and Spiritual Growth* copyright © 1978 by M. Scott Peck, M.D. on pages 95 and 96 are reprinted by permission of Simon & Schuster Adult Publishing Group, Inc. All rights reserved.

Excerpts from *Open Marriage* copyright © 1972 by Nena and George O'Neill are reprinted by permission of M. Evans and Company and The Rowman and Littlefield Publishing Group.

Marriage and Morals copyright © 1929 by Bertrand Russell was published by Horace Liveright. Excerpts reprinted by permission of Liveright Publishing Corporation, W.W. Norton & Company, Inc., The Bertrand Russell Peace Foundation Ltd., and Taylor & Francis.

The interview with Scott Peck by Robert Epstein entitled "Wrestling with God" was first published in *Psychology Today,* November/December 2002.

8 *Fly Fishing through the Midlife Crisis* copyright © 1993 by Howell Raines was published by Doubleday.

11 Norman MacLean's observation about the nature of grace and art is from his novella *A River Runs Through It* copyright © 1975 by Norman MacLean. Published by the University of Chicago Press.

Alden Nowlan's collection of poems *The Things Which Are* copyright © 1962 by Alden Nowlan was published by Contact Press. The phrase is from the King James Version of the Book of Revelation.

16 The excerpt from *Walden* copyright © 1854 by Henry David Thoreau was drawn from the version published by Penguin in 1983.

American Bloomsbury copyright © 2006 by Susan Cheever was published by Simon and Schuster.

Making for Home

7 Paul Goldberger's article, "Shanghai Surprise," was first published in the December 26, 2005, edition of the *New Yorker.* Excerpts reprinted by permission of the author.

12 *The Age of Unreason* copyright © 1989 by Charles Handy was published by Harvard Business School Press. Excerpts reprinted by permission of the publisher.